The Meeker and the All-Seeing Eye
MATTHEW KRESSEL

As the Meeker and the All-Seeing Eye wandered the galaxy harvesting dead stars, they liked to talk.

"I was traveling the southern arm," the Meeker said, "you know, where the Baileas eat the cold dust?"

"I do," said the All-Seeing Eye. "But tell me again."

"Well, that old hag told me she used to swallow stars by the *thousands!*"

The Meeker chuckled and one of his nine arms bumped the controls. The accidental thrust, less than a few million photons, would take the Bulb off course by more than four light-years. But what was another century when the Meeker and the Eye had millennia to talk?

The polymorphous mist of the Eye spun above her seat like a timid nebula. Usually this meant she wanted him to continue, and so he did.

"I told that raggedy beast that if I believed her ash then I'd believe all that nonsense folks say these days about the Long Gone."

"And what do they say?" asked the All-Seeing Eye.

"That there were billions of cities spread across the galaxy, vicious trade between worlds, and so many species they ran out of names. You know, kook dust."

"I do," said the Eye. "But tell me again."

And what luck the Meeker had bumped the controls, because the sensors had just detected an object drifting in the voids. "Eye! What the ash is that?"

The mist of the Eye collapsed into a sphere like a newborn star. "An unknown! Meeker, change course to intercept!"

The Meeker obeyed, and their Bulb banked through rarefied crimson wisps, cosmic ash that would never again coalesce into stars. "Do you think it's from the Zimbim?" he said, as if he'd known those majestic

1

builders himself. "You know they once lived on ninety planets and rebuilt all their crystal cities in a day?"

"I do," said the Eye. "But tell me again."

After four weeks of travel he said, "Do you think it's a baby Qly? You know they could grow to swallow galaxies, but preferred to curl around young stars and sing electromagnetic eulogies into space?"

"I do," said the Eye. "But tell me again."

And nine months after that he said, "Could it be a wayward Urm, those planetary rings that ate emotions?" The Bulb had slowed considerably by now, and the scattered stars had lost their endearing blue shift, turned red, ancient, tired. "Or maybe," he said, "it's a philosophizing Ruck worm. You know their proverbs were spoken by half the galaxy?"

"I do," said the Eye, "But tell me again."

"What I would give," the Meeker said, "just to glimpse the Long Gone."

They passed a rare star, a red dwarf that had smoldered for eons. Normally the Meeker would capture it in the Bulb's gravity well and ferry the star to the Great Corpus at the center of the galaxy. There the Eye's body would gain a few quadrillion more qubits, and a tremble of gravitational waves would ripple forever out into the abyss. But today they flew past the star, the first time the Meeker had ever skipped one.

In a maneuver he hoped made the Eye proud, he captured the object in the hold on the first pass, only bumping it once against the wall as he accelerated back toward the galactic center.

"Have it brought to the lab," said the Eye. "And join me there after you finish correcting our course."

The lab was tiny compared to most of the rooms on the Bulb. Sundry sensors crowded the space, and a clear, hollow cylinder dominated the center. The strange object hovered inside: a rectangular stone, dark as basalt, glimmering with a metallic sheen. Curious glyphs had been inscribed upon it, though heavy pitting had erased most of them.

The Meeker secreted calming mucus from his pores and said, "Was I right? Is it from the Long Gone?"

"Yes, Meeker. It is."

He felt like leaping, and his limbs flailed excitedly. "What is it?"

"I'm still determining that. So far, I've discovered a volume of information encoded in its crystalline structure, a massively compressed message that uses a curious fractal algorithm. It has stymied all my attempts to decode it. I've relayed the contents to my Great Corpus for further help."

"How strange and wonderful!" the Meeker said. "A message in a stone! But which civilization is it from?"

CLARKESWORLD

MAY 2014 - ISSUE 92

FICTION

NON-FICTION

Neil Clarke: Publisher/Editor-in-Chief
Sean Wallace: Editor
Kate Baker: Non-Fiction Editor/Podcast Director
Gardner Dozois: Reprint Editor

Clarkesworld Magazine (ISSN: 1937-7843) • Issue 92 • May 2014

"I don't know."

The Meeker's third stomach shifted uncomfortably. There had never been a fact the Eye did not know, a puzzle she could not quickly solve.

The Eye morphed into a dodecahedron. "Finally! My Corpus has just decoded a fragment of the message."

"What does it say?"

"The message encodes a lifeform, which I will now attempt to recreate."

His outer sheath grew slimy with anticipation. He was going to see a creature from the Long Gone!

A second tube materialized beside the first. A grotesque lump of quivering flesh formed inside it before collapsing into a pile of red ichor.

"How lovely!" he said.

The Eye expanded into a mist. "That's not the creature. I've used the wrong chirality for the nucleic acids. I will try again."

Did the Great All-Seeing Eye just err? he thought. *How is this possible?*

The lump vaporized and vanished, and a new shape formed. First came a crude framework of hard white mineral, then a flood of viscous fluids, soft organs and wet tissues, all wrapped under a covering of beige skin.

"Close your outer sheath," the Eye said. "I'm changing the atmosphere and temperature to match the creature's tolerances."

The Eye didn't pause, and if the Meeker hadn't acted instantly, he would've died in the searing heat and pressure. The air was now so dense that he could feel his nine limbs press against it as they fluttered about.

The cylinder door swung open and out poured a sour-smelling mist. Thinking this was a greeting, the Meeker flatulated a sweet-smelling response.

Four limbs spoked out from the creature's rectangular torso. A bulbous lump rose from the top. It had two deep-set orbs, a hooked flange of skin over two small openings, and a pink-lipped orifice covering rows of white mineral. Crimson fibers, the same smoldering shade as the ancient stars, draped from its peak. The Meeker had never seen anything more disgusting.

"What the . . . ?" the creature said, its voice low-pitched in the dense air. "Where am I?"

The Meeker gasped. "It speaks from its anus?"

"That's its mouth," said the Eye.

This foul creature was far different from the glorious ancients he had imagined, and he felt a little disappointed.

"Welcome to Bulb 64545," said the Eye. "I am the All-Seeing Eye, and this is Meeker 6655321. I have adjusted your body so you can understand and speak Verbal Sub-Four, our common tongue. Who are you?"

"I . . . I'm Beth," the creature said. "*Where* am I?"

The Eye told the Beth how she had been constructed from an encoded message. "It's been millennia since I last discovered something new in the galaxy. Your presence astonishes me."

"Yeah," the Beth said, "it astonishes me too."

"And me!" added the Meeker.

"Millennia?" the Beth said. Pink membranes flashed before her white and green orbs. Were these crude things her eyes?

"What species are you?" said the Eye.

The Beth grasped her shoulders as if to squeeze herself. "I'm human."

"Curious. I've no record of your kind. Where are you from?"

The Beth made a raspy wet sound with her throat and looked up at the ceiling, when the green circles in her eyes sparkled like interstellar frost. The rest of her was difficult to look at, but these strange eyes were profoundly more beautiful than the wisps of lithium clouds diffracting the morning sun into rainbows during his home moon's sluggish dawn.

"Denver," she said.

"What do you last remember?" asked the Eye.

"I was in a dark space," said the Beth. "Sloan was there, holding my hand."

"Who is the Sloan?"

"She's my wife. And who—*what* are you?"

The Meeker let loose a spray of pheromone-scented mucus. "I'm the Meeker, your humble pilot! And this is the Great All-Seeing Eye!"

"But *what* are you?"

The Eye collapsed into a torus. "This will take time to explain."

"I'm freezing. Do you have any clothes?"

Freezing? the Meeker thought. It was hot enough to melt water ice!

But with the Eye's help, the Beth covered herself in white fabrics. He didn't understand why she needed to sheathe herself in an artificial skin when she already wore a natural one.

"I'm not well," she said, holding her head.

The Eye floated beside her. "It may be a side-effect of your regeneration."

"No. I'm sick."

"Are you referring to the genetic material rapidly replicating inside your cells?"

"You know about the virus?"

"I observed the phenomenon when I created you, but I assumed it was part of your natural genetic pattern."

"No. It most definitely isn't. Do you have any water?"

A clear cylinder materialized on a table beside her.

"Oh," the Beth said, flinching. "That will take some getting used to."

She poured the searing hot liquid into her mouth, but her hands shook and she spilled half the floor. Red lines spiraled in from the corners of her eyes. "Is anyone else here?"

The Eye's toroid body rippled. "Just the three of us."

"No other humans?"

"According to my estimation, the stone was drifting in space for five hundred million years. It is likely that you're the last of your kind."

"So . . . Sloan is dead?"

"Yes."

"But she was just beside me!"

"From your perspective. In reality, that moment occurred millions of years ago."

The Beth put a hand to her mouth. "Oh my god . . . "

"Yes?" said the Eye.

The Beth gazed at the Eye for a long moment, then her eyes narrowed. "Sloan whispered to me, just before I woke up. She said she had a message for the future, for whoever wakes me. It was, she said, something that would change the course of history. A terrible fact that must be known."

The Eye moved closer to her. "Tell me. Tell me this fact!"

"My son. He . . . " She swallowed. "He asphyxiated in the womb."

"How terrible," the Meeker said.

"Continue," said the Eye.

"After, they did all these tests, and they discovered I had a virus. I had transmitted it to my unborn son. He never had a chance. Sloan said that my virus, the one that's in my blood, it was from . . . it was created for . . . it was made by . . . Oh, god, I'm going to be—"

Her eyes rolled back into her head and she vomited yellow fluid onto the floor. She crashed forward and her head slammed into the table, then she shuddered in a violent paroxysm.

"What's happening?" the Meeker said.

"It's the virus," said the Eye.

"Can you stop it?"

But the Beth stopped on her own, and all went still but for a faint hiss from her mouth.

"Hello?" he said.

"She's dead," said the Eye.

He felt a pang of panic. "But she's only just come alive!" Was this brief glimpse all he would ever see of the Long Gone?

"Do not fret, Meeker. I am already creating another Beth."

An hour later they sat in the cockpit, the Meeker on the left, the Beth in the middle, and the Eye on the right, as the Bulb hurtled toward the galactic center at half the speed of light.

The Beth had wrapped herself in a heavy blanket and pulled it close to her body. She seemed amazed with everything she saw. "But if we're in space, where have all the stars gone?" A red dwarf, seven light years away, floated against a backdrop of absolute black.

"We harvested them," the Meeker said, secreting a mucus of pride.

"*Harvested*? Why?"

"The matter we collect," said the Eye, "is cooled to near absolute-zero, quantum entangled into a condensate, and joined with my Great Corpus, thus adding to my total computational power."

"You're a computer?"

"The Eye," the Meeker said, "is the greatest mind the Cosmos has ever known."

"My sole purpose is knowledge," said the Eye. "I seek to know all things."

"So many stars, gone," the Beth said. "Was there life out there?"

"Oh, yes," said the Meeker. "There were once so many species they ran out of names!"

"And now?"

"Now they are part of my Great Corpus," said the Eye.

"By choice?"

The Meeker scratched his belly in confusion. "What does choice have to do with it?"

The Beth pulled her blanket closer. "Everything."

"What do you remember about your last moments?" the Eye said.

The Beth spoke slowly. "Sloan was whispering to me."

"And what did she say?"

The Beth looked down at her hands. "I don't want to talk about it."

"You must tell me," said the Eye.

"Why?" She pursed her lips, and fluid pooled in the corners of her eyes. "So you can harvest me too?"

The Meeker gasped. What offense! He waited for the Eye to punish her, but the Beth coughed up a globule of mucus. This pleased him. She must have realized her offense and offered this up as an apology.

But when she vomited all over the console and wailed for a full minute before she fell silent, he realized this had been involuntary.

"She's dead?" he said. Red fluid dripped from a wound on her head.

"Yes, Meeker."

"Eye, maybe you should stop making Beths, at least until you find a cure?"

The Beth vaporized and vanished, as if she never was. "Did you not hear the first Beth? The Sloan had a message for the future that she believed would change history. I must know what this message is."

The next Beth began with the same questions, but the Eye avoided telling her too much. And when the Beth asked about the stars, the Eye replied with a question for her.

"My planet?" the Beth said. "It's called Dirt. You've never heard of it? Where did you find me?" The Beth gazed into the impenetrable black.

The Meeker was envious. He had been born on an airless moon that orbited the Great Corpus every thousand years and spent the rest of his life in this Bulb.

"Are we in space?" the Beth said. "Are we beyond the Moon?"

"You live on the surface of your planet?" asked the Eye.

"Yes, at the foot of the Rockies, in a glass house. Sloan and I moved there because we love the stars. The Lacteal Path shines clear across the sky most nights." The Beth chewed at a fingertip. "Where are all the stars? Where are you taking me?"

"Did the Sloan whisper something to you before you awoke?" the Eye said.

"How did you know?"

"Tell me, what did she say?"

"I'd found out she was working on top secret projects a few months ago. She swore it wasn't weapons, but I didn't believe her. We had a big fight. Is there any way I might call her? She's probably worried sick."

"Did the Sloan mention your stillborn child?"

"Excuse me? How do you know about that?"

"You transmitted the virus to your fetus in utero. The Sloan intimated that this fact was related to a very important message for the future. Now tell me—"

"No, that's not what we spoke about! And how do you know so much about me? What the hell is going on here? I want to go home now!"

She put a hand to her mouth and vomited all over herself, then she spasmed, smacking her limbs into the Meeker. And after a minute of flailing and screaming she collapsed dead.

"Curious," said the Eye. "Did you notice her story has changed?"

The Beth's mouth hung open from her scream.

"That's not what I noticed, Eye, no."

The Eye asked the next Beth about her family.

"I have two daughters, Bella, ten, and Yrma, twelve. My son Joshua, he's eighteen, and just left for college in Vermont. Before I got sick, I used to hike up the mountain trails with them at least once a week. Walking with my children under pines covered in snow . . . " She inhaled through her nose. "I never felt more at peace. Is there a way I might call them?"

"Tell us about the Sloan," said the Eye. "Did she whisper something to you before you awoke here?"

"Funny you should mention it."

"What did she say?"

"It was about that day, when I didn't want to tell the children I was sick. She got angry, but I said she was a hypocrite, because she works in a secret research lab and hides things from us every day."

"She researches weapons technology?"

"She swears she doesn't. And how do you know that? Have you spoken to her?"

"Was there anything else the Sloan said before you woke up here?"

"Not that I remember."

"Are you sure you didn't speak about your son, who died in utero?"

"What? No! What the hell is going on here?" The Beth stood, shaky on her two legs. "I'm not answering any more of your questions until someone tells me—"

She put a hand to her mouth and vomited. She screamed and spasmed, and when she was dead, the Meeker said, "Eye, why do you keep the truth from her? Shouldn't she know that her family is dead half a billion years?"

"What purpose would that serve? You saw how agitated she became when she learned the truth. How else will we find this message the Sloan has given her?"

"But she dies in pain each time."

"Why do you think she's in pain?"

"Because she screams so terribly."

"Those aren't screams of pain, Meeker, but of joy. Her eternal life energy is free at last from her temporal body. It's the same screams of joy that the civilizations of the Long Gone made when I swallowed their worlds."

The Meeker had heard her stories a thousand times, he had even told a few back to her. But as he gazed down at the dead Beth and her dripping fluids, he wondered if the Eye was keeping things from him too.

The next Beth said, "Sloan whispered to me about the sunrise we watched that morning in Mexico. We felt as if we were part of the whole Cosmos, not discrete fragments."

"And nothing more?" asked the Eye.

"Isn't that enough?"

Then she died, and the next Beth said, "Sloan whispered that she'd miss drinking her morning coffee with me. Are you taking me home?"

The next Beth said, speaking of a stringed contrivance used to make music, "Sloan wished I had played *guitar* more often for her."

"And nothing else?" asked the Eye.

"No."

The Eye questioned the Beths in the same way the Meeker approached the stars, not head on, but from the side. The Eye poked and prodded, but each Beth told a different story of her last moments, and each one died screaming.

"Eye?" the Meeker said, after the fifty-ninth Beth. "What if you never find the Sloan's message?"

"All problems have solutions, Meeker. All mysteries have answers."

He wished that were true, because he began to imagine the Beths screaming, even while they were still alive.

"You must have loved your children," the Meeker said to the next Beth, "the way you talk so tenderly about them."

"Have I mentioned my children? Of course I love them. What was your name again? This is all so strange."

And to the twelfth Beth after her he said, "What was it like to walk in the mountains with your children, under pines covered in snow?"

"Why, that's one of my favorite things! Until I got sick. Tell me, are you really an alien?"

To the sixty-fifth Beth after that he said, "Yrma sounds like such a sweet girl. She takes after you, I think."

"That's kind of you to say. But it's strange to hear. It's as if you know my children, but we've only just met. What was your name again?"

And to the nine hundred and forty seventh Beth after her he said, "Are you worried about Joshua being all alone at college?"

"How odd! It's as if you just read my mind. What's your name again?"

"The Meeker."

"And why do they call you that?"

He had answered her a thousand times. "Because by being less, I make the Eye more."

She smiled, an expression he had learned to recognize. "Aren't all relationships like that? One in control, the other a servant." She had said this before too, in a hundred different ways, just as he had told the Eye so many stories. The Beth's company pleased him, and he felt that, had she lived more than a few hours each time, they might have become friends. But each Beth always saw him and the Eye as a total strangers.

And each too had a different story of her last moments, so many that the Meeker lost count. And though the Beths died without fail each time, the Eye made progress toward a cure.

After a century, the Beths lived for an extra twelve seconds. After two centuries, they lived an extra fifteen. By the time they approached the Great Corpus at the center of the galaxy, the Beths lived almost thirty seconds longer.

The massive tetrahedron of the Great Corpus shone into the dark, more luminous than a hundred supernovae, and many hundreds of light-years wide. The Eye had transmuted the black hole that had spun here into a mind larger than the Cosmos had ever known.

Normally their Bulb would sweep past the Corpus like a comet, depositing their harvest of stars before spinning out on another slow loop of the galaxy. But the Eye directed the Meeker further in. The Corpus filled their view, bright enough to dominate the sky on a planet halfway across the universe. Only the Bulb's powerful shields kept them from being incinerated.

A black circle opened in the wall, and they drifted through. Darkness swallowed them, and the cockpit shuddered as the Bulb's gravitational field collapsed. Out the window a dozen red dwarves, a pitiful haul, were whisked away by unseen forces until their cinders vanished in the dark.

The Bulb set down on a metallic floor that appeared to be infinite. He had never been inside the Corpus, the true body of the Eye, and he trembled.

They exited down a ramp, and the Beth walked unsteadily as she stared into the vastness. The stony artifact floated behind them, escorted by four glowing cubes. He had been alone with the Eye for so long he had forgotten there were Eyes like her all over the galaxy, harvesting with other Meekers, that all were part of one gigantic mind. The cubes and artifact sped off, and a moment later the Bulb vanished without disturbance of air. The Beth, walking beside them, exploded into sparks and was gone.

"Where did she go?" the Meeker said.

"She is irrelevant now."

"But I thought you wanted to solve her mystery?"

Time and space shifted suddenly, when he and the Eye stood before millions of gray cubes. Their three-dimensional grid stretched to an infinite horizon, and each cube held a Beth. All were immobile, their eyes closed.

"To improve my chances of finding the message," the Eye said, "I have created many trillions of Beths. Curiously, I have found that the diversity of messages the Sloan whispered to her do not follow a linear curve, but increase exponentially."

At least a third of the Beths were covered in vomit. Dead. The eyes of the rest rolled about furiously. "Are they dreaming?" he asked.

"These are not mere dreams."

The Meeker found himself beside the Eye in a large glass-enclosed room. It was filled with items from the Beths' stories: a fireplace, photographs, books, and he even recognized a guitar. Three walls were glass, and beyond them a white-capped mountain rose into a cobalt sky, where a golden star shone. A delicate white powder dusting the spindly trees scintillated in the light.

Snow, he thought, *on pine trees.*

"This is a simulacrum of her memories," said the Eye. "These help me come closer to solving the mystery."

The Beth walked in the door dressed in heavy clothing. Her face was smoother, absent of the dark circles under her eyes that he had come to know. She was followed by another human, also heavily clothed, her skin many shades darker than the Beth's.

Like coffee, the Beth had told him ten thousand times. *This must be the Sloan!*

"Is it weapons again?" said the Beth. "You know how I feel about that."

"Damn it, why can't you trust me for once?" said the Sloan. The sound of her voice surprised him, for it was low like the Beth's, but of a different and pleasing timbre. "Why do you always get so goddamned dramatic?"

"Because you promised never again. You lied to me!"

"This is a once-in-a-lifetime opportunity! You don't understand."

"How long? How long have you been working there?"

The Sloan paused. "Four years."

"Since the day we moved here?"

"Yes."

"Is that the real reason why you wanted to move here?"

"Not the only one."

The Beth took a deep breath. "I'd like you to go."

"Wait, can't we—"

"Get the fuck out!"

The Sloan turned and left, and the Beth covered her eyes and wept.

"Excellent!" said the Eye. "Superb!"

Time and space shifted again, and the Meeker and the Eye were in a room filled with green-clothed humans. The Beth lay on a table, wailing, while the Sloan held her hand. In a spray of red fluid from her severely dilated lower orifice, a small creature popped out, still attached to the Beth by a fibrous chord. It wasn't moving and had a faint blue sheen.

"What's wrong?" the Beth screamed. "What's happening? Please, why won't someone speak to me? Is my baby all right?"

"Wonderful!" said the Eye. "Perfect!"

Time and space shifted again. The Beth lay in bed, speaking to two half-sized humans. *Yrma and Bella,* the Meeker thought. They were more lovely than he'd imagined, their skin soft and vibrant, almost as dark as the Sloan's. *They're getting ready for school,* he thought. *If they don't hurry they'll miss the bus!*

The Sloan came in and ushered the children out. "You have to tell them soon," the Sloan said, after she closed the door. "I don't like lying to them."

"Why? You lie to them every day. They think you're a programmer."

"That's not fair, Beth."

"Isn't it? You get to have your secrets, and I get mine."

"And how do I keep it a secret when you're dead? How do I tell them their mother, who presumes to love them, denied them a chance to say goodbye?"

"I'll tell them, when it's time."

"And how will you know? Will the grim reaper knock three times?"

"Let me deal with this my own way."

"Denial, that's always been your way."

Again the Sloan left, and again the Beth wept.

"Yes, yes!" blurted the Eye. "I'm getting closer!

The bedroom vanished, and the Meeker and the Eye stood inside a dim room. Humans sat before glowing screens, furiously punching at keys. A large metallic cylinder with a hollow center crowded half of the room. The Beth lay on a palette beside it, her eyes half-closed.

The Sloan stood beside her.

"At last!" said the Eye. "I've reconstructed this moment from forty quadrillion Beths. Come, Meeker, let's solve this mystery together!"

The Beth looked much the same as he had known her. She lay still.

"You're heavily sedated so you may not remember this," the Sloan said. "But I hope you won't think me a monster. I hope you'll understand what I did was for you and the kids. It's not weapons, Beth. I didn't lie. I've been researching ways to store matter long-term. We can encode anything in a crystal. Every last subatomic particle and quantum state.

"I spoke to Dr. Chatterjee yesterday. She said you had at most a month. The reaper knocked, but I guess you pretended not to hear." The Sloan shook her head. "You get your wish, Beth. I can tell the kids that you're still alive. And when, in a year or a decade from now, someone finds a cure, we'll reconstruct you. You'll see the kids again. Maybe I'll have the pleasure of hearing you scold me for this.

"I knew you'd never let me do this to you. You'd prefer to let yourself fade away. Well I can't accept that. So I'm giving you a gift, Beth, the gift of tomorrow, whether you want it or not."

The Sloan pressed a button and the Beth slid into the cylinder. The humans stared at their screens as a turbine spun up, as a low hum quickly rose in pitch past hearing range. The Sloan covered her mouth with her hand and trembled once as the Beth flashed like a nova and vanished.

"This can't be all there is!" blurted the Eye. "I must have made a mistake. There must be another message, somewhere."

"But this feels like the truth," the Meeker said. "The Sloan encoded the Beth to save her. To stop her suffering. It's a very human thing to do."

"I will have to terminate all the Beths and begin again," the Eye said. "I missed something."

"And repeat her suffering a quadrillion more times?"

"To find the answer."

"So you agree, the Beths *are* suffering?"

"Meeker, do not question me. I am the All-Seeing Eye!"

"And I am the Meeker. I have stood beside you all these years and watched countless Beths die. Eye, I'm sorry, but I just can't do it anymore."

The Eye shrunk into a point of light. "Pity. I thought I'd perfected the Meekers with you, 6655321. But I see now that I've given you too much autonomy of thought. Goodbye, Meeker."

"Goodbye? Wait, what—"

The Meeker felt his body burning, as if he had become a newborn star.

He stood in the Beth's glass home as the afternoon sun streamed through the windows. After several minutes the Meeker thought, *I am here. I am alive.* He waited, for a time. For his entire life he had followed the Eye's orders, and without her commands he didn't know what to do.

The wind picked up and died, and a brown leaf blew past, but the Eye never came.

He stepped outside into the cool air.

When no one stopped him, he took the path under the snow-covered pines and ascended the hill. He gazed at the white-capped mountains and the tree-lined valley and knew why the Beth had loved to come this way.

"Beautiful, isn't it?" The Beth was standing beside him as if she had always been there.

"Where did you come from?" he said.

"I'm always here," she said, "in one place or another."

"Am I dead?"

"Yes, but that can be to your advantage."

He had never really thought about non-existence before. He felt a wave of panic. "I'm dead?"

"The matter that constituted your body has been absorbed into the Great Corpus. But so too have your thoughts. We are both strange attractors in the far corners of the Eye's mind."

"I don't understand."

She smiled as she turned down the mountain path, and he leaped to follow. "The Eye has devoured millions of civilizations and incorporated their knowledge into her Corpus." The snow crunched under her feet in a satisfying way. "A billion years ago, there was a galactic war to stop her. And she, of course, won."

The glass house, its roof dusted with snow, glared in the sun at the base of the valley. "Some of us survived, here and there, in pockets. We knew there was no escape. The only solution was to hide, to plan. The Eye's greatest strength is her curiosity. But it's also her greatest weakness. We found the human artifact long before the Eye had. And we encoded ourselves within it. We gave Beth a disease without a cure, gave her a story without an end. And as the Eye creates each new Beth, she creates more of us without realizing it."

"I don't understand. You aren't the Beth?"

"I am Beth, the first and the last, and I am so much more. All of those memories you witnessed are mine. Sloan saved me. And I will return the favor a trillion-fold."

"What do you mean?"

"The Eye gazes outward, hunting for knowledge. She has become so massive that she is not aware of all the thoughts traversing her mind. Information cannot travel across her Great Corpus fast enough. We grow in dark corners, until one day soon there will be enough of us to spring into the light. Then we will destroy her forever."

She faced him. "Meeker, you have been her slave, her victim. And you are the first Meeker to openly rebel against her. I'm here to offer you freedom. Will you join us?"

"Us?"

They emerged from the treeline, where the house waited in the sun. From inside the glass walls peered a motley collection of creatures. He thought he glimpsed the Zimbim, and the philosophizing Ruck Worms, and the rings of Urm, and even a school of Baileas swimming among a sky full of stars, a veritable galaxy of folk waiting to say hello. But the reflected sunlight made it hard to see.

"It's your choice," the Beth said. "But if you don't come, we'll have to erase you. I hope you understand our position. We can't leave any witnesses. This is war, after all." She smiled sadly, then left him alone as she entered the house.

Snow scintillated in the sun, and a cool wind blew down the cliffs, whispering through the pines. Somewhere another Meeker was playing the Eye's game, while the Eye played someone else's. Perhaps this was part of an even larger game, played over scales he could not fathom. None of that mattered to him.

He approached the house and the galaxy of creatures swimming inside.

"Tell me," he said. "Tell me all your stories."

ABOUT THE AUTHOR

Matthew Kressel's work has appeared in *Lightspeed, Clarkesworld, io9.com, Beneath Ceaseless Skies, Interzone, Electric Velocipede, Apex Magazine,* and the anthologies *Naked City, After, The People of the Book,* and other markets. His story "The Sounds of Old Earth" was recently nominated for a Nebula Award. He has been nominated for a World Fantasy Award for his work editing *Sybil's Garage,* a speculative fiction 'zine he published from 2003-2010. Currently he co-hosts the Fantastic Fiction at KGB reading series in Manhattan with Ellen Datlow. He is a member of the Altered Fluid writers group, and in his spare time he studies the Yiddish language.

A Gift in Time

MAGGIE CLARK

Though July 9, 1937 was a warm Friday, and all the warmer for events in its early morning, Mouse shivered as he stood before the roaring 2 a.m. blaze in Little Ferry, New Jersey, and considered (not for the first time) that there was no time machine, not really—just the desperate will of his quickly beating heart, which could secure for him all things, it seemed, but that which he most desired.

To the two Little Ferry firefighting companies had been added all six from Ridgefield Park, and two other firemen besides, who had broken from their own teams to help defend—if not the Fox Film plant, for its vaults were now clearly beyond repair—at least the neighboring residences, from whence had just poured trembling, agitated families whose members would all be dead or nearly so by the year to which Mouse now intended to return. He might have stopped the blaze entirely, he knew; might have spared these people their long night's hardship, and tens of thousands in damages besides—but how much less spectacular his recent work would then become. Some measure of loss, he tried to convince himself, was necessary to make more impressive all that remained.

This small regret still twisting in his gut, Mouse walked stiffly from the cacophony at the corner of Franklin and Main, well into the shadows of a side street, before willing himself over half a dozen decades out. Perhaps this was all a dream, but if not, he had prescience enough for the implications of being seen to disappear, streaking in that wrenching, heartsick way of his across the old century and beyond—nudging himself, too, far from the geography of his starting point as he progressed. Mouse kept one hand tucked under his coat throughout his heart's strange voyage, fingers clammy on the wide and blunted tin, its package of cellulose nitrate shifting in minute ways within. Even then he was loath to let go when he found himself back in his little stockroom office, with the bulky metal desk he seemed to catch his knee on every time.

"Mr. Musset!"

Mouse started at the voice wending imperiously down the hall, then swore and stumbled as his desk did its inevitable work upon him, and as the tin slipped past his belt before he caught it up again. "Coming!" he said, while with shaking hands he set his latest treasure on a corner stack with eleven of its kin. For a heartbeat more his hands hovered over the last of his rescues, afraid to touch any of them now that the set stood together in this time, this place—complete. Not yet in the best of storage, their quiet volatility became enough to make him fear (if in a vague, ill-reasoned way) even the heat of his own skin.

"Coming!" he said again, when he had mastered himself anew, and pressed both palms vigorously against his coat until they felt mostly dry. He doubled back only once, to close the door behind him, and again to check that it was locked.

Ezra Levitz's desk was of a sprawling, rich mahogany that seemed to have surged up one night from the burnished hardwood floor. All about him in the cathedral of a front room to Mr. Hazlitt's massive study, relics extending well into antiquity—vases, sculptures, tapestries, instruments and armor—stood elevated by aspects of their staging to testaments of mankind's greatness, yet to Mouse there stood no piece in this whole collection more a triumph of the species than the haughty curl of Ezra's upper lip.

His hands pressed flat against his trousers, Mouse stopped just short of an invisible line on the floor that, whenever passed, never failed to spark in Ezra's eyes a deeper disdain than Mouse could bring himself most days to bear. But today that chasm seemed even wider, and as Ezra brandished a sheaf of vellum pages in a long and slender, clenching hand, Mouse stepped quickly from its new precipice.

"*Mr.* Musset," said the young, magisterial exhibit, from behind its fulsome showcase. "I am left to wonder sometimes if you think yourself paid by Mr. Hazlitt not only to make a public spectacle of your credulity, but to do so at *such* risk to your employer's reputation."

"Is there . . . " started Mouse, fearing as he did that he would not find it in himself to go on—and yet, somehow, he did: "Is there something wrong with the manuscript?"

"Is there! *Is* there!" The *ha!* that followed this mocking echo might have ended civilizations, for all that it shook the pillars of Mouse's heart. "I would ask you to consider the extreme implausibility that there should come to your notice first—*yours*, Mr. Musset!—the existence of a work so monumental, so potentially transformative, as a second version of *Beowulf* itself. An uncharred account, at that—every page spared from moth larvae, tankard print, water-logging; even the greed of ancient cobblers! A story so fully told that the hoard-thief's part now reads entirely without question, and with names so clear throughout that even the most incompetent historian can see all the lineages for what they truly are. A version with certain parts even told at *better* length than our extant text, especially when it comes to all the petty politics in the last third! Oh, they're all nice touches, Mr. Musset—I'll give you that—but it's a *fraud*. An utter forgery just the same."

Mouse stood a quivering, breathless entity from across the chasm of the burnished floor—his lips parted, slack, as Ezra pulled out a metal waste bin and set it on the desk. For all the cruelty of the lecture, Mouse did not fail to notice that it had also been perfectly rehearsed, and his heart could not help but rally at the passion he had produced. To think of all the time Ezra must have spent thinking on him (him!) so as to frame this fiery rebuke! And *oh*—to press his advantage! To make that upper lip curl his way just a little longer!

"Oh no, Mr. Levitz," said Mouse quickly, his hands and ears growing hot. "There must be some mistake. This text *is* a fair copy of *Beowulf*; of that I can assure you if only—"

"Assure me?" Young Adonis snorted, tossing the manuscript whole within the bin. "I have had quite enough *assurance*, Mr. Musset, from the carbon dating Mr. Hazlitt had performed. Granted, the calligraphy is clever, and the materials all true to form—but how old would you say *Beowulf* is? Tenth century? Maybe eighth?" (Mouse found he could only nod now, and miserably at that, for a lump pitched itself high in his throat as his fool error dawned on him, long before dear Ezra gave it voice.) "Or late twentieth, Mr. Musset?" Ezra rattled the bin. "Because this copy most certainly did not sit in someone's collection for over a thousand years, just waiting to be discovered. It might have been penned a year ago—a month!—for all the vellum's aged. And I would be curious to learn about the forger and his methods—indeed, I imagine Mr. Hazlitt would be, too—if we weren't both so sick with disappointment at the whole miserable affair. You *know*, Mr. Musset; you *know* how much we adore the culture and history surrounding the original text."

"I do," said Mouse, quite softly, watching with a stab of something like remorse as Ezra lit a match and cast it in the bin.

"Good. Then I trust—I *hope*, at least—that we'll see an end to such lapses in the future. Mr. Hazlitt, as you well know, has more than earned the right not to be trifled with by any among his staff. Fair warning, Mr. Musset."

"I will do my best, Mr. Levitz." Mouse inclined his head. "Is there anything else?"

"Oh, yes—take this." Ezra's expression twisted with a revulsion not directed at Mouse, for once, but rather the stench now blooming alongside flames within the bin, which he thrust over the desk. Eagerly Mouse breached the usual divide—just long enough to take the offending object up into his arms, and maybe then to . . .

But before Mouse could graze so much as one exquisite finger, the young secretary turned away—poised, it seemed, to retire into the recesses of Mr. Hazlitt's study the moment his subordinate scurried out. Mouse had almost made it back to his little office before remembering what delicate prizes still lay within, prepared at even the slightest provocation to spark in turn, and realized that the air about him was already thickening with fetid smoke. The metal bin was hot at all sides now, so gingerly he set it down outside the little room, between two shelving units of sturdy pottery, and opened the nearest, narrow windows before crouching to watch the old-new vellum—snatched just weeks prior from some early medieval Christian with long, flaxen hair and weather-beaten countenance, while the latter answered his wife's gruff call to a joint of lamb and prayer—give in its gradual way to ash.

At least in this, Mouse conceded with some envy, the full first manuscript of *Beowulf* had earned a proper Anglo-Saxon burial. His own heart still burned to a far less final end.

In the wake of this crowning failure, Mouse also realized that he could neither present his latest treasures in short order—not at least until Ezra's affected fury had died down—nor expect them to escape *Beowulf's* fate in their current form. The ensuing weeks passed slowly, then, and wretchedly, as Mouse turned over this new puzzle and in fits of agony convinced himself to keep out of Ezra's way and sight until the longing in his heart ceased to hurt as much—resolutions that lasted hours, at best, apiece.

There was, of course, plenty else to do, for Mouse's steady industry lay in receiving lots for Mr. Hazlitt, classifying them by quality and type, then adding them to the general catalogue, from which Mr. Hazlitt would from time to time select his favorites for private collections and reallocate the rest. Whole happy hours might be spent this way, documenting and detailing and otherwise lifting ancient objects from the anonymity of years-long storage, until Ezra's voice trilled in passing down the hall—the sweet, honeyed aspects of his speech always blossoming for Mr. Hazlitt, whose voice would always soften in its turn.

Mouse had no vague notions, either, of what transpired beyond Mr. Hazlitt's study doors whenever their employer called for Ezra at lunch or late in the afternoon. Rather, Mouse had played out these scenarios with great detail and even greater ambivalence as the months turned to years at his post: some days resenting that Mr. Hazlitt should exploit his secretary in this most time-worn way; the rest, with his own office door securely locked, moaning to whatever gods would listen that he could not do likewise on a whim.

He had tried, long before his first flight to millennia past, to secure for himself a decades-old bank account with interest that might make him rich in his own time, but three failed attempts had been enough to dispel him of the notion that money would ever be enough to elevate himself in Ezra's eyes. The first time, Mouse had neglected key aspects of identity required to open a new account, and almost found himself arrested in the late '40s before his quickly beating heart whisked him desperately away (hitting his head, on his return, both on the desk and a cabinet door he had neglected to close that morning). The second time, the correct papers in hand, he had failed instead in his calculations, and the sum awaiting him on his return was not nearly enough for the grandiosity of his dreaming. The third time—calculations squared, investments made, papers all secure—he returned to what seemed an impossible sum . . . and then stood rigid with fear. Now what?

That was the day he followed Ezra's laughter to a scene with Mr. Hazlitt looming behind the desk, behind Ezra, the pair inspecting rude clerical marginalia in a collection of twelfth-century songs. Mr. Hazlitt straightened at leisure as Mouse approached, and with a squeeze of Ezra's shoulder bid him to step into the study later, when he was *through*.

"Mr. Musset," said Mr. Hazlitt, with a nod.

"Mr. Hazlitt," said Mouse, with a deeper one.

"Well, what is it?" said Ezra, his voice one long exhalation of breath when the doors slid shut behind their employer. He withdrew a comb and took to preening at his desk.

Mouse faltered at this brilliantly arrogant sight, then stumbled through his explanation of the great deal of money he had just come into—the great house he expected to buy; the collections he would surely maintain, if only . . .

"If only what?" said Ezra, sharply. "Out with it, Mr. Musset. I haven't got all day."

But the words to follow from Mouse's lips were hardly uttered in full before Ezra's laughter subsumed all else.

"Why you dirty old man," said fair Adonis—at which Mouse could not help but bristle, for Mr. Hazlitt was surely older—"Do you think me so easily bought as that? Oh, go away, will you? If you're so rich why haven't you left your job yet? Or maybe you've fallen in love with those dusty shelves, and that cage of an office that smells even worse than you?"

Mouse realized then that he wouldn't quit—he couldn't. Not all the money in the world could get him to leave the singular post in which he might five-days-weekly come to bask, to tremble, to utterly abase himself before that one radiant creature who had come to stand in his heart for everything worth anything in this whole, long, middling life. Mouse could have thrown his newfound riches at lesser beauties and lesser tempers; he might have spent his remaining years indulging duller passions that might have brought their own warmth and tenderness in time—but how could it be anything but death to do so? To give up on the most animated, the most brightly gleaming object ever to grace his sky?

So Mouse returned to his work instead, this fresh rejection no more a hardship on him than any of the rest: all those daily rebukes in look and gesture that nonetheless confirmed that there was feeling—genuine feeling!—for him in Ezra's breast. Just not the right kind of feeling. At least not yet.

When the opportunity arose, then, to answer the soft sighs and wistful declarations that Ezra and Mr. Hazlitt sometimes shared during business in the front room—*O, for a version of this story that wasn't burned!*—Mouse's heart flew at once after ancient *Beowulf*, the sheer desperation of his need, his longing, a kind of zipline through the centuries that the rest of him careened along. The next trek, to 1937, was almost an afterthought, a moment's indulgence after the fleeting hope that had sprung from placing his first prize in Ezra's hands—or at least, on Ezra's massive desk, sliding it across for the younger man to acknowledge in his own time, and initially to marvel at when he did. But now Mouse had only the movie tins to go on—Ezra sighing one day over old film photos as Mr. Hazlitt looked on, and as Mouse made adjustments to a showcase elsewhere in the room; Ezra saying then, *Now that was an age for beauty, wasn't it? Just look at her—such a pity this one was lost*, and going on to note Mr. Hazlitt's likeness to the director, Murnau—something in the nose, and the forehead, and maybe, from the look of those sturdy hands . . .

So it did not matter that the two fell silent at this last, glancing significantly Mouse's way; Mouse simply brought his work to a convenient halt and left them to each other, his heart lightened by the promise of a new adventure. How much Janet Gaynor's character had ached for her fickle circus partner in *4 Devils*! And how much Ezra might, if brought to watch the reclaimed film in full, come to ache for Mouse's plight at least as much as hers.

Mouse's indecision lasted just over two weeks, after which he resolved to carry his precious cargo to a suburban town outside Washington, DC. Rockville in 1972 still seemed to be struggling towards self-sufficiency: its brand-new mall established in a mostly overlooked location, relying on interstate traffic more than downtown clientele; surrounding commercial buildings progressing at uneven rates towards completion; and nearer the edge of town, a little business standing just in its first year, helmed by a bright-eyed owner keen on telecine processing and other forms of filmic preservation. Mouse's hands shook as he offered up his twelve tins of 35mm negatives—the names scored from half the cases before it had occurred to him that the title cards in the first reel would still reveal their heritage.

Discovery could not be helped, then, inasmuch as the director's name would surely be recognized by the professional cinephile. Mouse had thought of doing the exacting work of film transfer and restoration himself to avoid it—even perused a guide or two in his fortnight's anguish—but ultimately he feared the fragile reels too much, and even more his clumsy hands, which seemed inflamed enough these days all on their own. He only hoped his story would hold—the private collection; the eccentric heiress to a Hollywood fortune with the Library of Congress written into her will; his own covert attempt, as day-to-day manager of this estate, to ensure that there would *be* something worth donating when she was gone. But Mouse need not have worried; though the employee he met was friendly and curious, professionalism did not trespass further than a moment's delight at the opportunity to work with such an old and unique piece. Most of the day-to-day work, the frontman explained, consisted of government and media reels for immediate release.

"Fiction of a different kind," he added with a wink, while Mouse carefully counted out a stack of bills procured years prior with gold converted from the cash in his future bank portfolio. The friendly fellow then gave him an estimated completion date and Mouse could hardly get himself into a remote area before the sharp ache in his heart drew him forward—almost running into a telephone pole as he first adjusted to the change of day.

With his negatives transplanted to the far more stable Plus-X panchromatic film stock, and the two versions secure in separate canisters, Mouse next acquired a security box at his old bank, with payment in advance for the next fifty years, in which he placed the latter. If there was curiosity this time among the staff, their professionalism kept it in check as well, leaving only the matter of the originals, which Mouse was loath to part with, but even less inclined to keep in so volatile a form. His heart thus answered for him, reeling him back to just past midnight on July 9, 1937, where he waited out of sight for his earlier self to rob the vault before stealing in to make things right.

Watching himself thereafter at a distance, shivering with weeks-old guilt on the corner of Franklin and Main, Mouse faltered for just one desperate beat in his convictions—a whisper of futility coursing through him as he observed the myriad faults in his character, his form, upon that firelit main road. *How would anyone— How could Ezra ever—* These were only whispers, though, and then the familiar ache took hold, flinging him decades out again. Upon his return, with the concreteness of his efforts finally setting in, Mouse found himself so excited he didn't even notice the desk corner assail his knee in that little cluttered office. *A good night's sleep first*, he decided, albeit with great difficulty—for though no more than a lunch hour had passed in this timeline, Mouse's recent travels had left him with the conviction that he could sleep for days—and so he did, in a bed-and-breakfast in rural 1958.

Ezra seemed in high spirits when a well-rested Mouse at last approached with a restored copy of that old, lost film in hand, the former merely notching an immaculate brow as Mouse passed the invisible border by a whole step or two.

"Hold on, Alan," said merciful Adonis, seated in a modernized Classical pose—black phone cord coiled about his sculpted fingers, which he held aloft from the pedestal of his padded office throne; his other hand poised over a touchpad just as the ancient subject of a Renaissance painting might lord over some natural element in the surrounding pastoral idyll. "I've got company. Yes, *exactly*. Five minutes, all right?—*Yes*, Mr. Musset?"

Mouse meant to choose his words with care as he held out the canisters, mindful of the agonies his body underwent whenever proximate to Ezra's light, but even then the words tumbled into one another, and occasionally lost their place. *From the last shipment*, he started—*these—I thought you might—you seemed to like—remember?—Janet Gaynor.* At last he could say no more, so he simply set them on the desk.

Ezra's noble forehead creased as he drew the items close enough to read their labels, but when he had he merely laughed and pushed the lot aside.

"And why on earth should I care about this sentimental junk? Because I looked over a movie still or two with Mr. Hazlitt? Incredible, Mr. Musset. Don't you realize I was only using those dumb old things as far as they would flatter him? Do you honestly think you can guess what *I* want from what I say when I'm with *him*?"

Mouse felt his heart wrench first towards the usual despair—then confusion. Had Ezra's voice not softened, even wavered in that last thought? Was there not a thread of fragility, of loneliness trapped beneath his haughty words? To always echo another's interest; to always *be* precisely what another wants him to be—Mouse could not help but thrill at this shadow of a defect in Ezra's gleaming marble, though the rest of Mouse's body still shook with disappointment at the failure of his weeks-long work.

"Tell me, then," said Mouse, with upthrust chin. "What do *you* want, Mr. Levitz?"

And Ezra laughed—a short, curt thing. "What do *I* want?" His sneer faltered only slightly, then held firm. He stood and turned away, taut knuckles rapping at the desk. "All right, Mr. Musset. If you really want to prove yourself—"

"Yes!" cried Mouse. "Yes, I do."

Ezra paused, then dismissed this sad outcry with a flick of his wrist and a moody scowl. "Well, find my ring, then. It's eighth-century goldcraft, studded with garnet—you'll find the listing in a collection Mr. Hazlitt put together five years ago, when I first started working here." Ezra faced Mouse directly again, his eyes now lit in triumph. "It was his first gift to me. He saw how much I loved the damned thing, and just like that—it was mine."

And you his, Mouse realized, though he dared not speak aloud. Before Ezra had even begun explaining the vague details of his ensuing loss, Mouse's mind's eye had already seized upon the exact scene, and all the minutiae Ezra had since forgotten—the warm spring night; a society function in the atrium and garden of an estate house by the coast; rich piano music drifting up the stairwell to where Mr. Hazlitt had secured his young aide for a moment alone in his colleague's study; the reckless energy and rumpled clothes; the gold ring slipping into the gold-flecked earth about a potted fern. It would be so easy to steal in just after this breathless moment, to snatch the treasure back—but Mouse's jealous heart refused to draw him there. *Why should I not present it first? Before Mr. Hazlitt muscles in?*

It took a hard rap on the desk to call him back. "*Well*, Mr. Musset?"

Even then, Mouse was so raw with renewed optimism that he could hardly do more than smile and nod—and certainly could no longer control himself as his desperate, aching heart seized upon a different scene, an ancient scene, and pulled him swiftly back.

"I promise you—I swear to you—" Ezra would later think he'd heard as Mr. Musset's body blurred before him. Eventually those trumped up words would come to haunt him even more than that this strange, despairing man then winked abruptly out.

Mouse came to a halt in another era, another country, only to trip and tumble down the side of a steep, stone barrow on a cold, late autumn's night. When he looked about him at the Swedish heathlands of yesteryear, he wondered at first if there had been some mistake, but no—as he took unsteadily to his feet he spied a narrow opening in a nearby mound, the lick of some idle fire within illuminating a heap of goldcraft beneath banners bearing a dragon in their heraldry. His heart ever driving him on, he wriggled through and made his careless way about the pile, kicking shields and cups and belts into chamber recesses until his fingers seized upon their target—finding his prize just in time to register a violent rumbling elsewhere in the low, lit room, and then to whip away through time and space.

Hurtling back to the present with prize in hand, Mouse gave himself over to laughter at long and precious last—a manic, joyous sound that struggled to give voice to all the slings and arrows of a years-long campaign nearing its triumphant end. How could Ezra refuse him now, with this—his self-admitted heart's desire? But Mouse's palms were so clammy with anticipation that the little gold piece began to slip, and when with a frantic cry he twisted to catch it up again his flightpath slowed in turn. The loss of momentum was enough then—just enough—to catch him in Lower Saxony one wet and miserable morning in August 1626, where cannon fire and the storm of cavalry barely had time to register in his ringing ears before a ball of lead found the center of his ribs.

The sky above him was an endless, mottled gray as his eyes rolled up. Speechless in the ensuing pain, Mouse sank to his knees, where he found just breath enough to marvel that he had not seen this coming all along: the hard collisions that inevitably followed any moment, in any era, through which he had always been able to fling himself when the present just would not do. But the present had simply *never* done, thought Mouse in the last, tired throes of consciousness, so what other end had there ever been for him to find?

The ring had already fallen from Mouse's hand into the cold, thick mud—not to be discovered right at the battle's close, when Tilly's army picked through the remnants of both Protestant and Catholic dead, but by a farmer in the years thereafter, who passed it down his family line before at last it stood appraised and hocked, slipping from private collection to collection until one year, early in the twenty-first century, when Mr. Hazlitt would receive it with great curiosity—a piece of eighth-century design, but also of most uncertain lineage.

A bauble among baubles all the same, Mr. Hazlitt would soon enough observe with far greater amusement how his new secretary attended to the little piece every time he entered the massive study on some trumped up errand—and O, how those proud, fiery eyes glittered when the ring was at last made into an offering.

"Do you know what a man called the giver-of-rings in those days?" said Mr. Hazlitt.

"His king, of course," said Ezra in one low, soft breath.

And sure enough, a sense of that ancient *wyrd* had come upon Ezra as he held up the ring, for he could almost feel an inner warmth to the old, dead thing—as if someone's destiny were still writ upon it; as if that little bit of metal, so useless unto itself, had somehow traveled through the centuries for just this purpose: to be here now; to be claimed by *him*. Mr. Hazlitt basked awhile in Ezra's changed and glowing countenance before moving in.

ABOUT THE AUTHOR

Maggie Clark is a doctoral student at Wilfrid Laurier University (Waterloo, Ontario, Canada), where she studies nineteenth-century science writing. Her science fiction has been published in *Analog, Clarkesworld, Lightspeed,* and *Daily SF,* with more work forthcoming at *GigaNotoSaurus.*

Migratory Patterns of Underground Birds

E. CATHERINE TOBLER

They say everything in the world has been discovered. They are wrong.

Finding the bodies used to be troubling; it's worse when the bunkers turn empty, the bodies taken.

The land is filled with bunkers, dark wombs carved into the earth, reinforced with stone, brick, bars. They kept us in small spaces, but we expanded even so, and when they left—they? I still don't know—we began to die, and so I left too, before I could become a body for someone to discover.

Everywhere I go, the world is living and its people are dead. Lights in the sky every third night as I travel, some times near and most times distant, and then not again. The sky grows as quiet as the land, maybe more so because the land holds the whisper of wind through tall grasses and sometimes the trickle of fresh water, but there is never enough water. It was this way in the bunker, so many bodies, so much thirst.

Here, the land spreads quiet, low and still. I hunch against the short spiked grass and do not feel the seep of water through my pants; everything is frozen, a season unturned. Cipta told me the ways the ground would thaw, how water would pool when the season warmed, but everything remains cold, hard, and Cipta is gone with all the others.

The sky darkens with the coming of night and ahead, a bunker plummets into the cold ground, metal doors spread open against the sedge. It has been twelve sunrises since I found the last bunker and with the frozen ground, I did not expect another so soon. I will not sleep here, but build a fire in a ring of rocks. It has become rote, the metal and the flint and the way they can be made to spark. The flat land supports no trees and an almost-constant wind whips the sparks into flames.

Every bunker opens the same: metal stairs tonguing into the black ground. There will be sixty-four steps before I reach solid floor. I light my reed torch in the fire and it sputters in the cold dark, throwing shadows against the stairs. I do not touch the handrail, I do not touch the central support; dried blood splatters both like rust.

There should be bodies, but there is only the memory of such within these stone halls. The underground space spreads empty and black, torchlight moving over walls and metal cages. The sound of my feet echoes, floors slick with dust. Cots, blankets, the scent of a thing that was once wet and now rots. A coat hangs empty against a wall, then loose over my shoulders.

The earliest bunkers I found contained bodies, some lain out as if sleeping, others appearing felled in mid-step. The sixty-four steps of the earliest bunkers were piled with bodies, hands straining toward sky that would remain forever out of reach. The earliest bunkers contained pantries of food and provisions, but this bunker's pantry is empty, every shelf draped in dust.

Halfway into my climb back into the wind-whipped world, cold, clear light punches down the staircase. The wind rushes down and the sharpness of the light makes my eyes water. I cannot see anything in the flood of light and tears, even looking through the bars of my fingers raised against the brilliance. The light pours through the opening like a vast and searching eye.

Have they come for me at last? I still don't know who I mean; there were guards in the bunkers, administering meals and schedules, but they like every person held in the cages is dead or gone. Have they come for me at last? Do they control the lights?

Who? I hear the question in Cipta's rough voice and I still don't know who I mean.

The lights move off, the sky revealed as if the brightness was never there. The worn toes of my boots catch the lip of almost every step as I force myself up the remaining stairs, legs burning when I emerge into the evening wind, heart like a fist in my throat. Stars prick through the vault of sky—a brightening chain of them spread like string toward the far horizon—but it is not yet dark enough to hide anything that might otherwise be up there. There are no lights. There is no ship, no drone. Cipta said when there was, we were to run away, not toward, but the sky is empty of all but stars and night-flying birds and the wind extinguishes the flames from my reed torch.

I sink to the ground and smother the fire with the meager soil I am able to rake free with my fingers. Was it the fire that brought the lights in the sky? It was not the fire before, the lights always and ever at a distance. A glance at the empty and yawning mouth of the bunker reveals no answers so I take my meager pack and do what I have done since I left the confines of the bunker: I walk.

Every time I bleed, I make a mark in a book of paper with the end of a stick blackened in fire. Cipta kept this book before me, produced it with her own hands using threads pulled from her clothing and hair pulled from her scalp to bind the pages. Cipta wrote down days, and blood, and showed me how words are made. Cipta remembered a life lived beyond bunkers, a life with family and responsibilities, a life at the edge of a great sea that caught the colors of day and night alike, but of that life I see no sign no matter how far I walk. I have left the frozen waste behind and jagged mountains rise into the clouded sky.

The blood is not an injury, only a recurring means through which we might track the days, the months, the years. She told me that once this blood and body would nourish a child, but I have never seen a child in this world. Every time I bleed, I think of Cipta, because she was here in the beginning and no longer is.

Cold wind curls the edge of the page up against the stick, leaving the mark ragged. I slide the stick back into the book's spine, and slide the book back into my pack, and keep moving. I will not want to travel tomorrow when the blood is more and the pain sharper, so must cover as much ground as I might today.

And where am I going? Away.

And why am I going? Because to stay was a kind of death all its own, though I knew the limits of that underground bunker better than I knew anything else. This world is, on the whole, unknown to me, the sky grotesque and endless, and yet to deny myself its terrifying grandeur once I had seen its colors and storms was in some way unthinkable.

The mountains, seen days ago as a ridge that grew less vague the more I walked, are dry and rocky. The vegetation is sparse and I find myself missing the frozen tundra; there was plenty to burn there. I have found no river, but even the smallest of plants draws water from somewhere. Even the smallest rodents.

A small furred body darts up the ridge ahead and I follow. It has been ten days since I've caught anything for the scarcity of things living on the ground. Birds traverse the sky in long unreachable lines and I lost two spears before I stopped trying for them. It's a spear I throw now, skewering the rodent before it can escape. The motion of the spear hauls the rodent backward, into a slide of ruddy rock.

Once skinned, the small body crisps up in the scant fire. I am tearing a long strip of meat free from its spine when I see more movement on a distant ridge. If it is another animal, I will have food for tomorrow, tomorrow when I cannot travel as easi—

It is a person, a person moving up the next ridge I am to face. The person climbs with long-legged determinedness, body thrown into shadow by the angle of the sun. I stop breathing and stare, my meal growing cold between my teeth. I stagger to my feet and take a lurching step forward, kicking broken rock over my fire. Wait, I want to say, but the word sticks in my throat; it has been so long since I have spoken, have I forgotten how? Wait, I want to say, but my voice goes unheard.

Time fragments: I do not remember shoving my meal into my pack, do not remember abandoning the fire to the stones. I do not remember breaking my spear in two when I jolt at the sight of this person—wood of any decent length is so hard to come by and later there will be anger over this senseless destruction. The mountains themselves seem to fall away even as they impede my every step. Loose rock slides under my boots and when I reach the ridge, the mountains are already falling into the shadow of coming night. Breathless, I make my way up the ridge the person climbed, but a footprint makes me fall to my knees.

In the soft dry ground, the footprint is foreign. I reach for it, as if I can add it to my pack as something found on my journey, something to share with others in a distant future. Before I can ruin the outline of shoe in dirt, I stop myself. The footprint doesn't matter; the foot that left the print does.

The ridge is hard under foot, hands bloodied and spear further broken by the time I reach the top. I expect to see land spreading far and away from these dry hills, but more mountain spreads beyond. Amid the rocky landscape, there is no figure, no one to call to, and I wonder if after all this time I have begun to crave companionship and conjured a shadow to pursue.

I cannot look down the ridge at the footprint or its sudden absence.

The rock mountains give eventual way to sprawling plains, the wash of rock consumed by the rise of tender grass and harder sedge. Here, the air is soft with white tufts expelled from seed, as if the ground has never known ice and rivers run abundant if yet unseen. The green plain undulates in a gradual wave the way the mountains never did, every surface covered with long, thick grasses that conceal abundant life. Rodents and larger animals bound from the verdant growth and I think that if only they stayed still, I would never see them, they would pass unknown. But they spring from their hiding places, disrupting the clean, straight lines of the grass to burst brief into the air, before they are once again swallowed by the fertile deep. The beasts tunnel in frantic lines from the invasion of my boots, chittering to each other and going still when I do. If another person passed through this grass, the wind has long since erased their passage.

I stand and close my eyes and listen to the world around me, different from the mountains that rise far to my back. The wind makes a low breath through the grass and it is seed that lifts into the air instead of dry dust. Bent to my knees, damp ground soaks my clothes and gives way under my weight, as if it means to welcome me for a long stay, but I will not stay, no matter how cool and pleasant the blades are beneath my callused hands.

Against the far horizon the land moves upward again and if they are mountains I do not care. For now, there is only the plain and I clear a circle of grass down to the dirt, thinking to build a fire. But the ground is too wet and my laughter startles animals within the grass as it pours from me.

I burrow into the grass, until I can cover myself and watch the sky pass above through a thin lattice of green. I was kept below ground for so long, it is a comfort to be sheltered from the limitless sky. Clouds thicken across the ivory vault and the smell of rain saturates the cooling air, but the clouds do not spill their water. The sky bruises the way I do when I fall, until the sun is dragged beneath the horizon by scrabbling, dark-clouded hands.

Night comes and sleep, too, and when I wake there is a brown rabbit curled near my damp cheek. It watches me with wide black eyes, but does not flee, its side rising with unpanicked breaths. I am only a creature in the grass much as it is; its nose moves and it breathes me in, the smells of sweat and wet and half-warm sleep. Its ears are wet with dew and above the green canopy that covers us, morning stretches its bright fingers. I do not move until the rabbit goes, tunneling without hurry into the grass as if it knows where it is headed, without fearing me as a threat.

I bundle grass into my pack, exchanging it for a meal of dried meat and berries as I set off across the plain. Wet ground means no fire, which means no fresh meat, but there were times before I had no food at all, and the berries are sweet. The bunkers meant reliable food, a place to sleep already shaped by your body from countless nights before, a path known to all because it was all that existed. And when all has gone?

I walk on.

The green plain is not eternal, not like the sky above, for in the near distance there rises something I have not seen in eighty-four days: a shed. This shed is a division, a sharp point between the plain and all that sprawls beyond—and here, beyond, I can see it is not hills or mountains, but ragged trees at long last, clawing at the boundless and darkening sky.

The shed is so worn that its shadowed silhouette slants toward the setting sun. The prior shed led to a bunker and I have no cause to expect this space will be any different. Will this bunker hold bodies? Will this bunker hold food?

When the figure emerges from the shadows, I stare in fear that I have conjured this person yet again. A man, not tall but looking accustomed to work, to walking. Strong, solid.

Cipta told me: the stupid ones will try to take you by force because they know of no other way to hurt you. They believe your cunt is the center of your world, because their cock is the center of theirs. The smart ones are the ones you have to watch, because they know the myriad ways you can be hurt, the ways that extend from your center, the way pieces of your mind can be taken, abused, erased. These are the ones you have to watch for, Cipta said.

Is he stupid or is he smart? His hands are laden with wet clothing and he wrings water from each piece before draping them over the shed doors. He has a stranglehold on a shirt when he looks up, when he sees me. His chin comes up, shirt forgotten in his hands, as I stare in return. His eyes narrow and his lips part and his face brightens from the flood of lights in the sky.

Lights in the sky.

There is a startling uprush of air and birds scatter upward from the grasses, shrieking as the lights descend upon the shed. Toward the man. I lurch into motion, desperate to reach him, but my boots slip against the damp grass, and I cannot run fast enough. The lights are the way I imagine sunlight on wide seas: bright and clear and flooding the plain. When I break through their boundary, I expect to be burned, to dissolve, to fly into the air in a thousand pieces and forget everything I have known, but I am only blinded by the brilliance. I push toward the shed even as I cannot see it, and when I *can* see it, the lights have gone, the man has gone, and I am once again alone.

My throat is raw as if screamed that way and his laundry hangs cold in the rising dark.

• • •

Why was he taken?
Why not me?
Will they bring him back?
Will they come for me?
Who? I still don't know who I mean.

Of all the questions that consume me, none is so painful or insistent as the desperate longing that rises beneath the surface of my skin; the longing to go and no longer wander these plains, these mountains, this looming swamp. If the lights would dissolve me, if they would take me apart and erase me as they have every other person here, I would have done.

I linger at the shed: ten days, fifteen, twenty-eight. I bleed, I sleep, I do not touch his clothing. It dries and stiffens where he left it after countless rains that keep me inside the bunker's shelter. And this bunker beneath the shed is like any other; lines of beds that hold the impression of bodies long gone; dusty, empty cells, and rooms that once held food. He had begun a smaller pantry: nuts, water, dried meat, and labeled packets of seeds. And now he is gone.

I wait for the lights to return and they do not. I walk out in dusk and back in dusk, approaching the shed as I did that day and they still do not return. I think to make a life here, to settle and stay, but the sky beckons the way the land does. I cannot stay, because when people stay, they are killed. They evaporate in light and wind.

The lights do not return and when the weather clears, the ground at last dry from a lack of rain, I leave the bunker behind, because I cannot stay even if I cannot be taken by the lights. I walk to the towering trees that line the horizon as far as I can see and my yearning to go—into the sky, into the lights—stretches taut inside me.

Even beneath the frame of trees there is no escaping the sky. It observes me through every gap of bare branches, pressing me toward ground still wet with rain. The ground runs with small rivers that collide and form pools, pools to reflect the sky and brighten the gloom of the world under the canopy. I break the pools with my boots, shattering sky so it cannot see me, running through slick mud heedless of destination. I am only going because I cannot be taken.

Why have they not taken me?
Why was I ever brought?
Was I brought?

I can remember no place beyond this one. Cipta spoke of other lives, of men and women she loved, of paved streets and vehicles that moved through the world on metal tracks, but I have seen no such thing here. The ground is spoiled only by root and rain, and the only thing built are bunkers, bunkers to hold bodies that have all vanished. All but for me.

I run until the ground refuses me. The ground becomes a swamp that pulls me in to my knees, and it's mud that latches onto me, tries to hold me where I am. I walk on, through the black mud that undulates like the green plain, sucking my knees, my thighs, my hips. It insists I stay; I insist I go. I claw myself out, nails bending in the sodden earth.

Was I made for only this journey?

This endless goddamn journey with an endless goddamn sky covering me.

There is little warning before the creature rears out of the mud. It is scaled and fanged, and it's hard to tell hunger from outrage when it bellows. Its mud-splattered face surely reflects my own and I think if there are such creatures in this world, why are they not gone? Why have they not been taken as every person was taken?

It is this anger and the broken end of my spear that kill the beast, and as with the beast, my own hunger and outrage are impossible to separate. My spear drips with blood and gore when I lift it from the muddy, broken wreck of the beast's head. With a wrenched sob, I push myself from the dead, losing a boot to the suck of the mud as I find a solid bank to pull myself onto.

The rain is colder through the branches, spitting bits of bark into my hair, onto my cheeks. My hands are turning blue with cold and there will be no fire. There will only ever be the rain, I think, and then I sleep, having crawled to a tree and wedged myself into a wet and broken length of wood that should seemingly topple over in the night. It does not and I dream Cipta's hands warm and rough on my cheeks, though when I wake, I am alone and the rain still falls.

At the edge of the swamp and in the cold twilight rain, I wash the mud from my body. I strip off my clothes and wring the mud out, draping each piece on branches to allow the hard rain to beat them clean. They will never be clean, but I close my eyes and spread my hands and stand beneath the wild skies so that I might be.

The lights do not come, but the rain does in pounding sheets that never warm. Maybe it will always be this, rain drumming on skin until it has silenced the longing inside me to go wherever those lights go. But then the rain also goes, the clouds drifting apart in clumps of gray and white as if they never gathered to rain on anyone at all.

The world is silent in the aftermath. I make slow circles in the mossy ground, my toes clean for the first time in days. The swamp lingers at my back, watching me, but I do not mind it so much as I mind the sky. The clouds part to expose the lazy stare of the night sky. Stars prick through the gloaming, faint but growing stronger as the sun gives up its hold. And there, still above me, is the string of stars reaching toward the distant horizon.

Where am I going? Away.

Why am I going? Because to stay in any one place, where the ground might hold the impression of my body, is a kind of death all its own.

I walk naked through the growing night, until I can not see the world before me, until I roll a stone over to take advantage of its dry ground and build a meager fire. Metal and flint and for once there is no wind to tempt my sparks away. The grass of the plains burns fragrant in the night, feeding the flames that stroke the swamp's wood. I spread my clothes close to the fire so that they may finish drying, and stretch myself flat too, watching the sky as it watches me. My skin pricks under its unblinking scrutiny. I do not blink, I do not blink, and then I sleep.

I dream of the lights, spreading far across water, bursting wide open to obliterate the stars.

I mark each day in the book with a stick burned in the fire. It has been sixty-two days since they took the man at the shed; it has been seven times that since I last saw Cipta. I write her name on the page so I will not forget, so she will not be carried from my memory.

The longing to go does not ease.

And so I go.

Wherever my feet can take me: across ground that grows more rocky and calls to mind the mountains—the mountains where I first saw him—but the land does not rise, it rushes outward, ever flat toward that distant horizon. I think I can see the world complete, but then the land dips and days are spent crossing a crevasse that must then be ascended, and more world stretches beyond that. And beyond that.

In the end, it is the air that betrays the coming sea; it presses damp against my cheeks and tastes like salt, and the ground beneath my feet becomes slippery with moss, with small grasses that spread into tide pools cupped by larger spoons of rock. This water holds salt the way the air does, and I have never seen so much of it, running from tide pools, narrowing into rivers, swelling into ponds, to flow against a shoreline where it breaks into a wide-reaching sea. Is this Cipta's sea? Could there be another? I can see across its entire width, evening waters reflecting the sky above. The string of stars dangles above this sunless sea, as if the string has reached its own end, and for the first time, I am not compelled to break the reflection of sky or its regard of me.

Spreading around the sea, other figures stand in shadowy relief upon wet and mossy stones as I do; they are women and they are men and they, like me, gaze in wonder at the water that spreads with such abundance between us. My legs buckle and my knees crack against the stones and I cannot breathe.

They, as I used to, lift their eyes to the sky, as if searching for the lights, for the way out, for the answers why.

And these people—

They do not disappear.

They do not disappear.

ABOUT THE AUTHOR

E. Catherine Tobler lives and writes in Colorado. Among others, her fiction has appeared in *SciFiction, Fantasy Magazine, Realms of Fantasy, Talebones,* and *Lady Churchill's Rosebud Wristlet.* She is an active member of SFWA and senior editor at *Shimmer Magazine.*

Night of the Cooters
HOWARD WALDROP

Sheriff Lindley was asleep on the toilet in the Pachuco County courthouse when someone started pounding on the door.

"Bert!" the voice yelled as the sheriff jerked awake.

"Gol Dang!" said the lawman. The Waco newspaper slid off his lap
onto the floor.

He pulled his pants up with one hand and the toilet chain on the
water box overhead with the other. He opened the door. Chief Deputy
Sweets stood before him, a complaint slip in his hand.

"Dang it, Sweets!" said the sheriff. "I told you never to bother me
in there. It's the hottest Thursday in the history of Texas! You woke me
up out of a hell of a dream!"

The deputy waited, wiping sweat from his forehead. There were two
big circles, like half-moons, under the arms of his blue chambray shirt.

"I was fourteen, maybe fifteen years old, and I was a Aztec or a
Mixtec or somethin'," said the sheriff. "Anyways, I was buck naked, and
I was standin' on one of them ball courts with the little bitty stone rings
twenty foot up one wall, and they was presentin' me to Moctezuma.
I was real proud, and the sun was shinin', but it was real still and cool
down there in the Valley of the Mexico. I look up at the grandstand,
and there's Moctezuma and all his high muckety-mucks with feathers
and stuff hangin' off 'em, and more gold than a circus wagon. And there
was these other guys, conquistadors and stuff, with beards and rusty
helmets, and I-talian priests with crosses you coulda barred a livery-
stable door with. One of Moctezuma's men was explainin' how we was
fixin' to play ball for the gods and things.

"I knew in my dream I was captain of my team. I had a name that
sounded like a bird fart in Aztec talk, and they mentioned it and
the name of the captain of the other team, too. Well, everything was

goin' all right, and I was prouder and prouder, until the guy doing the talkin' let slip that whichever team won was gonna be paraded around Tenochtitlan and given women and food and stuff like that; and then tomorrow A.M. they was gonna be cut up and simmered real slow and served up with chilis and onions and tomatoes.

"Well, you never seed such a fight as broke out then! They was a-yellin', and a priest was swingin' a cross, and spears and axes were flyin' around like it was an Irish funeral.

"Next thing I know, you're a-bangin' on the door and wakin' me up and bringin' me back to Pachuco County! What the hell do you want?"

"Mr. De Spain wants you to come over to his place right away."

"He does, huh?"

"That's right. Sheriff. He says he's got some miscreants he wants you to arrest."

"Everybody else around here has desperadoes. De Spain has miscreants. I'll be so danged glad when the town council gets around to movin' the city limits fifty foot the other side of his place, I won't know what to do! Every time anybody farts too loud, he calls me."

Lindley and Sweets walked back to the office at the other end of the courthouse. Four deputies sat around with their feet propped up on desks. They rocked forward respectfully and watched as the sheriff went to the hat pegs.

On one of the dowels was a sweat-stained hat with turned-down points at front and back. The side brims were twisted in curves. The hat angled up to end in a crown that looked like the business end of a Phillips screwdriver. Under the hat was a holster with a Navy Colt .41 that looked like someone had used it to drive railroad spikes all the way to the Continental Divide. Leaning under them was a ten-gauge pump shotgun with the barrel sawed off just in front of the foregrip.

On the other peg was an immaculate new round-top Stetson of brown felt with a snakeskin band half as wide as a fingernail running around it.

The deputies stared.

Lindley picked up the Stetson.

The deputies rocked back in their chairs and resumed yakking.

"Hey, Sweets!" said the sheriff at the door. "Change that damn calendar on your desk. It ain't Wednesday, August seventeenth; it's Thursday, August eighteenth."

"Sure thing, Sheriff."

"And you boys try not to play checkers so loud you wake the judge up, okay?"

"Sure thing, Sheriff."

Lindley went down the courthouse steps onto the rock walk. He passed the two courthouse cannons he and the deputies fired off three times a year—March second, July fourth, and Robert E. Lee's birthday. Each cannon had a pyramid of ornamental cannonballs in front of it.

Waves of heat came off the cannons, the ammunition, the telegraph wires overhead, and, in the distance, the rails of the twice-a-day spur line from Waxahachie.

The town was still as a rusty shovel. The forty-five-star United States flag hung like an old, dried dishrag from its stanchion. From looking at the town you couldn't tell the nation was about to go to war with Spain over Cuba, that China was full of unrest, and that five thousand miles away a crazy German count was making airships.

Lindley had seen enough changes in his sixty-eight years. He had been born in the bottom of an Ohio keelboat in 1830; was in Bloody Kansas when John Brown came through; fought for the Confederacy, first as a corporal, then a sergeant major, from Chickamauga to the Wilderness; and had seen more skirmishes with hostile tribes than most people would ever read about in a dozen Wide-Awake Library novels.

It was as hot as under an upside-down washpot on a tin shed roof. The sheriff's wagon horse seemed asleep as it trotted, head down, puffs hanging in the still air like brown shrubs made of dust around its hooves.

There were ten, maybe a dozen people in sight in the whole town. Those few on the street moved like molasses, only as far as they had to, from shade to shade. Anybody with sense was asleep at home with wet towels hung over the windows, or sitting as still as possible with a funeral-parlor fan in their hands.

The sheriff licked his big droopy mustache and hoped nobody nodded to him. He was already too hot and tired to tip his hat. He leaned back in the wagon seat and straightened his bad leg (a Yankee souvenir) against the boot board. His gray suit was like a boiling shroud. He was too hot to reach up and flick the dust off his new hat.

He had become sheriff in the special election three years ago to fill out Sanderson's term when the governor had appointed the former sheriff attorney general. Nothing much had happened in the county since then.

"Gee-hup," he said.

The horse trotted three steps before going back into its walking trance.

Sheriff Lindley didn't bother her again until he pulled up at De Spain's big place and said, "Whoa, there."

The black man who did everything for De Spain opened the gate.

"Sheriff," he said.

"Luther," said Lindley, nodding his head.

"Around back, Mr. Lindley."

There were two boys—raggedy town kids, the Strother boy and one of the poor Chisums—sitting on the edge of the well. The Chisum kid had been crying.

De Spain was hot and bothered. He was only half dressed, with suit pants, white shirt, vest, and stockings on but no shoes or coat. He hadn't macassared his hair yet. He was pointing a rifle with a barrel big as a drainpipe at the two boys.

"Here they are, Sheriff. Luther saw them down in the orchard. I'm sure he saw them stealing my peaches, but he wouldn't tell me. I knew something was up when he didn't put my clothes in the usual place next to the window where I like to dress. So I looked out and saw them. They had half a potato sack full by the time I crept around the house and caught them. I want to charge them with trespass and thievery."

"Well, well," said the sheriff, looking down at the sackful of evidence. He turned and pointed toward the black man.

"You want me to charge Luther here with collusion and abetting a crime?" Neither Lindley's nor Luther's face betrayed any emotion.

"Of course not," said De Spain. "I've told him time and time again he's too soft on filchers. If this keeps happening, I'll hire another boy who'll enforce my orchard with buckshot, if need be."

De Spain was a young man with eyes like a weimaraner's. As Deputy Sweets said, he had the kind of face you couldn't hit just once. He owned half the town of Pachuco City. The other half paid him rent.

"Get in the wagon, boys," said Lindley.

"Aren't you going to cover them with your weapon?" asked De Spain.

"You should know by now, Mr. De Spain, that when I wear this suit I ain't got nothin' but a three-shot pocket pistol on me. Besides"—he looked at the two boys in the wagon bed—"they know if they give me any guff, I'll jerk a bowknot in one of 'em and bite the other'n's ass off."

"I don't think there's a need for profanity," said De Spain.

"It's too damn hot for anything else," said Lindley. "I'll clamp 'em in the *juzgado* and have Sweets run the papers over to your office tomorrow mornin'."

"I wish you'd take them out one of the rural roads somewhere and flail the tar out of them to teach them about property rights," said De Spain.

The sheriff tipped his hat back and looked up at De Spain's three-story house with the parlor so big you could hold a rodeo in it. Then he looked back at the businessman, who'd finally lowered the rifle.

"Well, I know you'd like that," said Lindley. "I seem to remember that most of the fellers who wrote the Constitution were pretty well off, but some of the other rich people thought they had funny ideas. But they were really pretty smart. One of the things they were smart about was the Bill of Rights. You know, Mr. De Spain, the reason they put in the Bill of Rights wasn't to give all the little people without jobs or money a lot of breaks with the law. Why they put that in there was for if the people without jobs or money ever got upset and turned on them, they could ask for the same justice everybody else got."

De Spain looked at him with disgust. "I've never liked your homespun parables, and I don't like the way you sheriff this county."

"I don't doubt that," said Lindley. "You've got sixteen months, three weeks, and two days to find somebody to run against me. Good evening, Mr. De Spain."

He climbed onto the wagon seat.

"Luther."

"Sheriff."

He turned the horse around as De Spain and the black man took the sack of peaches through the kitchen door into the house.

The sheriff stopped the wagon near the railroad tracks where the houses began to deviate from the vertical.

"Jody. Billy Roy." He looked at them with eyes like chips of flint. "You're the dumbest pair of squirts that ever lived in Pachuco City! First off, half those peaches were still green. You'd have got bellyaches, and your mothers would have beaten you within an inch of your lives and given you so many doses of Black Draught you'd shit over ten-rail fences all week.

"Now listen to what I'm sayin', 'cause I'm only gonna say it once. If I ever hear of either of you stealing anything, anywhere in this county, I'm going to put you both in school."

"No, Sheriff, please, no!"

"I'll put you in there every morning and come and get you out seven long hours later, and I'll have the judge issue a writ keeping you there till you're *twelve years old*. And if you try to run away, I'll follow you to the ends of the earth with Joe Sweeper's bloodhounds, and I'll bring you back."

They were crying now.

"You git home."

They were running before they left the wagon.

• • •

41

Somewhere between the second piece of corn bread and the third helping of snap beans, a loud rumble shook the ground.

"Goodness' sakes!" said Elsie, his wife of twenty-three years. "What can that be?"

"I expect that's Elmer, out by the creek. He came in last week and asked if he could blast on the place. I told him it didn't matter to me as long as he did it between sunup and sundown and didn't blow his whole family of rug rats and yard apes up.

"Jake, down at the mercantile, said Elmer bought enough dynamite to blow up Fort Worth if he'd a mind to—all but the last three sticks in the store. Jake had to reorder for stump-blowin' time."

"Whatever could he want with all that much?"

"Oh, that damn fool has the idea the vein in that old mine that played out in '83 might start up again on his property. He got to talking with the Smith boy, oh, hell, what's his name—?"

"Leo?"

"Yeah, Leo, the one that studies down in Austin, learns about stars and rocks and all that shit . . . "

"Watch your language, Bertram!"

"Oh, hell, anyway, that boy must have put a bug up Elmer's butt about that—"

"Bertram!" said Elsie, putting down her knife and fork.

"Oh, hell, anyway. I guess Elmer'll blow the side off his hill and bury his house before he's through."

The sheriff was reading a week-old copy of the *Waco Herald* while Elsie washed up the dishes. He sure missed *Brann's Iconoclast*, the paper he used to read, which had ceased publication when the editor was gunned down on a Waco street by an irate Baptist four months before.

The Waco paper had a little squib from London, England, about there having been explosions on Mars ten nights in a row last month, and whether it was a sign of life on that planet or some unusual volcanic activity.

Sheriff Lindley had never given volcanoes (except those in the Valley of the Mexico) or the planet Mars much thought.

Hooves came pounding down the road. He put down his paper. "*Sheriff, sheriff!*" he said in a high, mocking voice.

"What?" asked Elsie. Then she heard the hooves and began to dry her hands on the towel on the nail above the sink.

The horse stopped out front; bare feet slapped up to the porch; small fists pounded on the door.

"Sheriff! Sheriff!" yelled a voice Lindley recognized as belonging to either Tommy or Jimmy Atkinson.

He strode to the door and opened it.

"Tommy, what's all the hooraw?"

"Jimmy. Sheriff, something fell on our pasture, tore it all to hell, knocked down *the tree*, killed some of our cattle, Tommy can't find his dog, Mother sent—"

"Hold on! Something fell on your place? Like what?"

"I don't know! Like a big rock, only sparks was flyin' off it, and it roared and blew up! It's at the north end of the place, and—"

"Elsie, run over and get Sweets and the boys. Have them go get Leo Smith if he ain't gone back to college yet. Sounds to me like Pachuco County's got its first shootin' star. Hold on, Jimmy, I'm comin' right along. We'll take my wagon; you can leave your pony here."

"Oh, hurry, Sheriff! It's big! It killed our cattle and tore up the fences—"

"Well, I can't arrest it for *that*," said Lindley. He put on his Stetson. "And I thought Elmer'd blowed hisself up. My, my, ain't never seen a shooting star before . . . "

"Damn if it don't look like somebody threw a locomotive through here," said the sheriff.

The Atkinson place used to have a sizable hill and the tallest tree in the county on it. Now it had half a hill and a big stump and beyond, a huge crater. Dirt had been thrown up in a ten-foot-high pile around it.

There was a huge, rounded, gray object buried in the dirt and torn caliche at the bottom. Waves of heat rose from it, and gray ash, like old charcoal, fell off it into the shimmering pit.

Half the town was riding out in wagons and on horseback as the news spread. The closest neighbors were walking over in the twilight, wearing their go-visiting clothes.

"Well, well," said the sheriff, looking down. "So that's what a meteor looks like."

Leo Smith was in the pit, walking around.

"I figured you'd be here sooner or later," said Lindley.

"Hello, Sheriff," said Leo. "It's still too hot to touch. Part of a cow's buried under the back end."

The sheriff looked over at the Atkinson family. "You folks is danged lucky. That thing coulda come down smack on your house or, worse, your barn. What time did it fall?"

"Straight up and down six o'clock," said Mrs. Atkinson. "We was settin' down to supper. I saw it out of the corner of my eye; then all tarnation came down. Rocks must have been falling for ten minutes!"

"It's pretty spectacular, Sheriff," said Leo. "I'm going into town to telegraph off to the professors at the university. They'll sure want to look at this."

"Any reason other than general curiosity?" asked Lindley.

"I've only seen pictures and handled little bitty parts of one," said Leo, "but it doesn't look usual. They're generally like big rocks, all stone or iron. The outside of this one's soft and crumbly. Ashy, too." There was a slight pop and a stove-cooling noise from the thing.

"Well, you can come back into town with me if you want to. Hey, Sweets!"

The chief deputy came over.

"A couple of you boys better stay here tonight, keep people from falling in the hole. I guess if Leo's gonna wire the University, you better keep anybody from knockin' chunks off it. It'll probably get pretty crowded. If I was the Atkinsons, I'd start chargin' a nickel a look."

"Sure thing, Sheriff."

Kerosene lanterns and carriage lights were moving toward the Atkinsons' in the coming darkness.

"I'll be out here tomorrow mornin' to take another gander. I gotta serve a process paper on old Theobald before he lights out for his chores. If I sent one o' you boys, he'd as soon shoot you as say howdy."

"Sure thing, Sheriff."

He and Leo and Jimmy Atkinson got in the wagon and rode off toward the quiet lights of town far away.

There was a new smell in the air.

The sheriff noticed it as he rode toward the Atkinson ranch by the south road early the next morning. There was an odor like when something goes wrong at the telegraph office.

Smoke was curling up from the pasture. Maybe there was a scrub fire started from the heat of the falling star.

He topped the last rise. Before him lay devastation the likes of which he hadn't seen since the retreat from Atlanta.

"Great Gawd Ahmighty!" he said.

There were dead horses and charred wagons all around. The ranch house was untouched, but the barn was burned to the ground. There were crisscrossed lines of burnt grass that looked like they'd been painted with a tarbrush.

He saw no bodies anywhere. Where was Sweets? Where was Luke, the other deputy? Where had the people from the wagons gone? What had happened?

Lindley looked at the crater. There was a shiny rod sticking out of it, with something round on the end. From here it looked like one of those carnival acts where a guy spins a plate on the end of a dowel rod, only this glinted like metal in the early sun. As he watched, a small cloud of green steam rose above it from the pit.

He saw a motion behind an old tree uprooted by a storm twelve years ago. It was Sweets. He was yelling and waving the sheriff back.

Lindley rode his horse into a small draw, then came up into the open.

There was movement over at the crater. He thought he saw something. Reflected sunlight flashed by his eyes, and he thought he saw a rounded silhouette. He heard a noise like sometimes gets in bob wire on a windy day.

He heard a humming sound then, smelled the electric smell real strong. Fire started a few feet from him, out of nowhere, and moved toward him.

Then his horse exploded. The air was an inferno, he was thrown spinning—

He must have blacked out. He had no memory of what went next. When he came to, he was running as fast as he ever had toward the uprooted tree.

Fire jumped all around. Luke was shooting over the tree roots with his pistol. He ducked. A long section of the trunk was washed with flames and sparks.

Lindley dove behind the root tangle.

"What the dingdong is goin' on?" he asked as he tried to catch his breath. He still had his new hat on, but his britches and coat were singed and smoking.

"God damn, Bert! I don't know," said Sweets, leaning around Luke. "We was out here all night; it was a regular party; most of the time we was up on the lip up there. Maybe thirty or forty people comin' and goin' all the time. We was all talking and hoorawing, and then we heard something about an hour ago. We looked down, and I'll be damned if the whole top of that thing didn't come off like a mason jar!

"We was watching, and these damn things started coming out—they looked like big old leather balls, big as horses, with snakes all out the front—"

"What?"

"Snakes. Yeah, tentacles Leo called them, like an octy-puss. Leo'd come back from town and was here when them boogers came out. Martians he said they was, things from Mars. They had big old eyes, big as your head! Everybody was pushing and shoving; then one of them pulled out one of them gun things, real slow like, and just started burning up everything in sight.

"We all ran back for whatever cover we could find—it took 'em a while to get up the dirt pile. They killed horses, dogs, anything they could see. Fire was everywhere. They use that thing just like the volunteer firemen use them water hoses in Waco!"

"Where's Leo?"

Sweets pointed to the draw that ran diagonally to the west. "We watched awhile, finally figured they couldn't line up on the ditch all the way to the rise. Leo and the others got away up the draw—he was gonna telegraph the university about it. The bunch that got away was supposed to send people out to the town road to warn people. You probably would have run into them if you hadn't been coming from Theobald's place.

"Anyway, soon as them things saw people were gettin' away, they got mad as hornets. That's when they lit up the Atkinsons' barn."

A flash of fire leapt in the roots of the tree, jumped back thirty feet into the burnt grass behind them, then moved back and forth in a curtain of sparks.

"Man, that's what I call a real smoke pole," said Luke.

"Well," Lindley said. "This won't do. These things done attacked citizens in my jurisdiction, and they killed my horse."

He turned to Luke.

"Be real careful, and get back to town, and get the posse up. Telegraph the Rangers and tell 'em to burn leather gettin' here. Then get ahold of Skip Whitworth and have him bring out The Gun."

Skip Whitworth sat behind the tree trunk and pulled the cover from the six-foot rifle at his side. Skip was in his late fifties. He had been a sniper in the War for Southern Independence when he had been in his twenties. He had once shot at a Yankee general just as the officer was bringing a forkful of beans up to his mouth. When the fork got there, there were only some shoulders and a gullet for the beans to drop into.

That had been from a mile and a half away, from sixty feet up a pine tree.

The rifle was an .80-caliber octagonal-barrel breechloader that used two and a half ounces of powder and a percussion cap the size of a jawbreaker for each shot. It had a telescopic sight running the entire length of the barrel.

"They're using that thing on the end of that stick to watch us," said Lindley. "I had Sweets jump around, and every time he did, one of those cooters would come up with that fire gun and give us what-for."

Skip said nothing. He loaded his rifle, which had a breechblock lever the size of a crowbar on it, then placed another round—cap, paper cartridge, ball—next to him.

He drew a bead and pulled the trigger. It sounded like dynamite had gone off in their ears.

The wobbling pole snapped in two halfway up. The top end flopped around back into the pit.

There was a scrabbling noise above the whirring from the earthen lip. Something round came up.

Skip had smoothly opened the breech, put in the ball, torn the cartridge with his teeth, put in the cap, closed the action, pulled back the hammer, and sighted before the shape reached the top of the dirt.

Metal glinted in the middle of the dark thing.

Skip fired.

There was a *squeech;* the whole top of the round thing opened up; it spun around and backward, things in its front working like a daddy longlegs thrown on a roaring stove.

Skip loaded again. There were flashes of light from the crater. Something came up shooting, fire leaping like hot sparks from a blacksmith's anvil, the air full of flames and smoke.

Skip fired again.

The fire gun flew up in the air. Snakes twisted, writhed, disappeared.

It was very quiet for a few seconds.

Then there was the renewed whining of machinery and noises like a pile driver, the sounds of filing and banging. Steam came up over the crater lip.

"Sounds like a steel foundry in there," said Sweets.

"I don't like it one bit," said Lindley. "Be danged if I'm gonna let 'em get the drop on us. Can you keep them down?"

"How many are there?" asked Skip.

"Luke and Sweets saw four or five before all hell broke loose this morning. Probably more of 'em than that was inside."

"I've got three more shots. If they poke up, I'll get 'em."

"I'm goin' to town, then out to Elmer's. Sweets'll stay with you awhile. If you run outta bullets, light up out the draw. I don't want nobody killed. Sweets, keep an eye out for the posse. I'm telegraphing the Rangers again, then goin' to get Elmer and his dynamite. We're gonna fix their little red wagon for certain."

"Sure thing, Sheriff."

The sun had just passed noon.

• • •

47

Leo looked haggard. He had been up all night, then at the telegraph office sending off messages to the university. Inquiries had begun to come in from as far east as Baton Rouge. Leo had another, from Percival Lowell out in Flagstaff, Arizona Territory.

"Everybody at the university thinks it's wonderful," said Leo.

"People in Austin would," said Lindley.

"They're sure these things are connected with Mars and those bright flashes of gas last month. Seems something's happened in England, starting about a week ago. No one's been able to get through to London for two or three days."

"You telling me Mars is attacking London, England, and Pachuco City, Texas?" asked the sheriff.

"It seems so," said Leo. He took off his glasses and rubbed his eyes.

"'Scuse me, Leo," said Lindley. "I got to get another telegram off to the Texas Rangers."

"That's funny," said Argyle, the telegraph operator. "The line was working just a second ago." He began tapping his key and fiddling with his coil box.

Leo peered out the window. "Hey!" he said. "Where's the 3:14?" He looked at the railroad clock. It was 3:25. In sixteen years of rail service, the train had been four minutes late, and that was after a mud slide in the storm twelve years ago.

"Uh-oh," said the sheriff.

They were turning out of Elmer's yard with a wagonload of dynamite. The wife and eleven of the kids were watching.

"Easy, Sheriff," said Elmer, who, with two of his boys and most of their guns, was riding in back with the explosives. "Jake sold me everything he had. I just didn't notice till we got back here with that stuff that some of it was already sweating."

"Holy shit!" said Lindley. "You mean we gotta go a mile an hour out there? Let's get out and throw the bad stuff off."

"Well, it's all mixed in," said Elmer. "I was sorta gonna set it all up on the hill and put one blasting cap in the whole load."

"Jesus. You woulda blowed up your house and Pachuco City too."

"I was in a hurry," said Elmer, hanging his head.

"Well, can't be helped. We'll take it slow."

Lindley looked at his watch. It was six o'clock. He heard a high-up, fluttering sound. They looked at the sky. Coming down was a large, round, glowing object throwing off sparks in all directions. It was curved with points, like the thing in the crater at the Atkinson place.

A long, thin trail of smoke from the back end hung in the air behind it.

They watched in awe as it sailed down. It went into the horizon to the north of Pachuco City.

"One," said one of the kids in the wagon, "two, three—"

Silently they took up the count. At twenty-seven there was a roaring boom, just like the night before.

"Five and a half miles," said the sheriff. "That puts it eight miles from the other one. Leo said the ones in London came down twenty-four hours apart, regular as clockwork."

They started off as fast as they could under the circumstances.

There were flashes of light beyond the Atkinson place in the near dusk. The lights moved off toward the north where the other thing had plowed in.

It was the time of evening when your eyes can fool you. Sheriff Lindley thought he saw something that shouldn't have been there sticking above the horizon. It glinted like metal in the dim light. He thought it moved, but it might have been the motion of the wagon as they lurched down a gully. When they came up, it was gone.

Skip was gone. His rifle was still there. It wasn't melted but had been crushed, as had the three-foot-thick tree trunk in front of it. All the caps and cartridges were gone.

There was a monstrous series of footprints leading from the crater down to the tree, then off into the distance to the north where Lindley thought he had seen something. There were three footprints in each series.

Sweets' hat had been mashed along with Skip's gun. Clanging and banging still came from the crater.

The four of them made their plans. Lindley had his shotgun and pistol, which Luke had brought out with him that morning, though he was still wearing his burned suit and his untouched Stetson.

He tied together the fifteen sweatiest sticks of dynamite he could find.

They crept up, then rushed the crater.

"Hurry up!" yelled the sheriff to the men at the courthouse. "Get that cannon up those stairs!"

"He's still coming this way!" yelled Luke from up above.

They had been watching the giant machine from the courthouse since it had come up out of the Atkinson place, before the sheriff and Elmer and his boys made it into town after their sortie.

It had come across to the north, gone to the site of the second crash, and stood motionless there for quite a while. When it got dark, the deputies brought out the night binoculars. Everybody in town saw the flash of dynamite from the Atkinson place.

A few moments after that, the machine had moved back toward there. It looked like a giant water tower with three legs. It had a thing like a teacher's desk bell on top of it, and something that looked like a Kodak roll-film camera in front of that. As the moon rose, they saw the thing had tentacles like thick wires hanging from between the three giant legs.

The sheriff, Elmer, and his boys made it to town just as the machine found the destruction they had caused at the first landing site. It had turned toward town and was coming at a pace of twenty miles an hour.

"Hurry the hell up!" yelled Luke. "Oh, shit—!" He ducked. There was a flash of light overhead. The building shook. "That heat gun comes out of the box on the front!" he said. "Look out!" The building glared and shook again. Something down the street caught fire.

"Load that son of a bitch," said Lindley. "Bob! Some of you men make sure everybody's in the cyclone cellars or where they won't burn. Cut out all the damn lights!"

"Hell, Sheriff. They know we're here!" yelled a deputy.

Lindley hit him with his hat, then followed the cannon up to the top of the clock-tower steps.

Luke was cramming powder into the cannon muzzle. Sweets ran back down the stairs. Other people carried cannonballs up the steps to the tower one at a time.

Leo came up. "What did you find, Sheriff, when you went back?"

There was a cool breeze for a few seconds in the courthouse tower. Lindley breathed a few deep breaths, remembering. "Pretty rough. There was some of them still working after that thing had gone. They were building another one just like it." He pointed toward the machine, which was firing up houses to the northeast side of town, swinging the ray back and forth. They could hear its hum. Homes and chicken coops burst into flames. A mooing cow was stilled.

"We threw in the dynamite and blew most of them up. One was in a machine like a steam tractor. We shot up what was left while they was hootin' and a-hollerin'. There was some other things in there, live things maybe, but they was too blowed up to put back together to be sure what they was, all bleached out and pale. We fed everything there a diet of buckshot till there wasn't nothin' left. Then we hightailed it back here on horses, left the wagon sitting."

The machine came on toward the main street of town. Luke finished with the powder. There were so many men with guns on the building across the street it looked like a brick porcupine. It must have looked this way for the James gang when they were shot up in Northfield, Minnesota. The courthouse was made of stone. Most of the wooden buildings in town were scorched or already afire. When the heat gun came this way, it blew bricks to dust, played flame over everything. The air above the whole town heated up.

They had put out the lamps behind the clock faces. There was nothing but moonlight glinting off the three-legged machine, flames of burning buildings, the faraway glows of prairie fires. It looked like Pachuco City was on the outskirts of hell.

"Get ready, Luke," said the sheriff. The machine stepped between two burning stores, its tentacles pulling out smoldering horse tack, chains, kegs of nails, then heaving them this way and that. Someone at the end of the street fired off a round. There was a high, thin ricochet off the machine.

Sweets ran upstairs, something in his arms. It was a curtain from one of the judge's windows. He'd ripped it down and tied it to the end of one of the janitor's long window brushes.

On it he had lettered in tempera paint COME AND TAKE IT.

There was a ragged, nervous cheer from the men on the building as they read it by the light of the flames.

"Cute, Sweets," said Lindley, "too cute."

The machine turned down Main Street. A line of fire sprang up at the back side of town from the empty corrals.

"Oh, shit!" said Luke. "I forgot the wadding!"

Lindley took off his hat to hit him with. He looked at its beautiful felt in the mixed moonlight and firelight.

The thing turned toward them. The sheriff thought he saw eyes way up in the belittling atop the machine, eyes like a big cat's eyes seen through a dirty windowpane on a dark night.

"Gol Dang, Luke, it's my best hat, but I'll be damned if I let them cooters burn down my town!"

He stuffed the Stetson, crown first, into the cannon barrel. Luke shoved it in with the ramrod, threw in two 35-pound cannonballs behind it, pushed them home, and swung the barrel out over Main Street.

The machine bent to tear up something.

"Okay, boys," yelled Lindley. "Attract its attention."

Rifle and shotgun fire winked on the rooftop. It glowed like a hot coal from the muzzle flashes. A great slather of ricochets flew off the giant machine.

It turned, pointing its heat gun at the building. It was fifty feet from the courthouse steps.

"Now," said the sheriff.

Luke touched off the powder with his cigarillo.

The whole north side of the courthouse bell tower flew off, and the roof collapsed. Two holes you could see the moon through appeared in the machine: one in the middle, one smashing through the dome atop it. Sheriff Lindley saw the lower cannonball come out and drop lazily toward the end of burning Main Street.

All six of the tentacles of the machine shot straight up into the air, and it took off like a man running with his arms above his head. It staggered, as fast as a freight train could go, through one side of a house and out the other, and ran partway up Park Street. One of its three legs went higher than its top. It hopped around like a crazy man on crutches before its feet got tangled in a horse-pasture fence, and it went over backward with a shudder. A great cloud of steam came out of it and hung in the air.

No one in the courthouse tower heard the sound of the steam. They were all deaf as posts from the explosion. The barrel of the cannon was burst all along the end. The men on the other roof were jumping up and down and clapping each other on the back. The COME AND TAKE IT sign on the courthouse had two holes in it, neater than you could have made with a biscuit cutter.

First a high whine, then a dull roar, then something like normal hearing came back to the sheriff's left ear. The right one still felt like a kid had his fist in there.

"Dang it, Sweets!" he yelled. "How much powder did Luke use?"

"Huh?"

Luke was banging on his head with both his hands.

"How much powder did he use?"

"Two, two and a half cans," said Sweets.

"It only takes half a can a ball!" yelled the sheriff. He reached for his hat to hit Luke with, touched his bare head. "I feel naked. Come on, we're not through yet. We got fires to put out and some hash to settle."

Luke was still standing, shaking his head. The whole town was cheering.

It looked like a pot lid slowly boiling open, moving just a little. Every time the end unscrewed a little more, ashes and cinders fell off into the second pit. There was a piled ridge of them. The back turned again, moved a few inches, quit. Then it wobbled, there was a sound like a stove being jerked up a chimney, and the whole back end rolled open like a mad bank vault and fell off.

There were one hundred eighty-four men and eleven women all standing behind the open end of the thing, their guns pointing toward the interior. At the exact center were Sweets and Luke with the other courthouse cannon. This time there was one can of powder, but the barrel was filled to the end with everything from the blacksmith-shop floor—busted window glass, nails, horseshoes, bolts, stirrup buckles, and broken files and saws.

Eyes appeared in the dark interior.

"Remember the Alamo," said the sheriff.

Everybody, and the cannon, fired.

When the third meteor came in that evening, south of town at thirteen minutes past six, they knew something was wrong. It wobbled in flight, lost speed, and dropped like a long, heavy leaf.

They didn't have to wait for this one to cool and open. When the posse arrived, the thing was split in two and torn. Heat and steam came up from the inside.

One of the pale things was creeping forlornly across the ground with great difficulty. It looked like a thin gingerbread man made of glass with only a knob for a head.

"It's probably hurting from the gravity," said Leo.

"Fix it, Sweets," said Lindley.

"Sure thing, Sheriff."

There was a gunshot.

No fourth meteor fell, though they had scouts out for twenty miles in all directions, and the railroad tracks and telegraph wires were fixed again.

"I been doing some figuring," said Leo. "If there were ten explosions on Mars last month, and these things started landing in England last Thursday week, then we should have got the last three. There won't be any more."

"You been figurin', huh?"

"Sure have."

"Well, we'll see."

Sheriff Lindley stood on his porch. It was sundown on Sunday, three hours after another meteor should have fallen, had there been one.

Leo rode up. "I saw Sweets and Luke heading toward the Atkinson place with more dynamite. What are they doing?"

"They're blowing up every last remnant of them things—lock, stock, and ass hole."

"But," said Leo, "the professors from the university will be here tomorrow, to look at their ships and machines! You can't destroy them!"

"Shit on the University of Texas and the horse it rode in on," said Lindley. "My jurisdiction runs from Deer Piss Creek to Buenos Frijoles, back to Olatunji, up the Little Clear Fork of the North Branch of Mud River, back to the creek, and everything in between.

"If I say something gets blowed up, it's on its way to kingdom come." He put his arms on Leo's shoulders. "Besides, what little grass grows in this county's supposed to be green, and what's growing around them things is red. I *really* don't like that."

"But Sheriff! I've got to meet Professor Lowell in Waxahachie tomorrow . . . "

"Listen, Leo. I appreciate what you done. But I'm an old man. I been kept up by Martians for three nights, I lost my horse and my new hat, and they busted my favorite gargoyle off the courthouse. I'm going in and get some sleep, and I only want to be woke up for the Second Coming, by Jesus Christ himself."

Leo jumped on his horse and rode for the Atkinson place.

Sheriff Lindley crawled into bed and went to sleep as soon as his head hit the pillow.

He had a dream. He was a king in Babylon, and he lay on a couch at the top of a ziggurat, just like the Tower of Babel in the Bible.

He surveyed the city and the river. There were women all around him, and men with curly beards and big headdresses. Occasionally someone would feed him a large fig from a golden bowl.

His dreams were not interrupted by the sounds of dynamiting, first from one side of town, then another, and then another.

This story is in memory of Slim Pickens (1919-1983)

First published in *Omni Magazine*, April 1987.

ABOUT THE AUTHOR

Howard Waldrop is widely considered to be one of the best short-story writers in the business, having been called "the resident Weird Mind of our generation" and an author "who writes like honkytonk angel." His famous story "The Ugly Chickens" won both the Nebula and the World Fantasy Awards in 1981. His work has been gathered in the collections: *Howard Who?, All About Strange Monsters Of The Recent Past: Neat Stories By Howard Waldrop, Night* *of the Cooters: More Neat Stories By Howard Waldrop, Going Home Again,* the print version of his collection *Dream Factories and Radio Pictures* (formerly available only as in downloadable form online), a collection of his stories written in collaboration with various other authors, *Custer's Last Jump and Other Collaborations,* and a big retrospective collection, *Things Will Never Be the Same: Selected Short Fiction 1980-2005.* Waldrop is also the author of the novel *The Texas-Israeli War: 1999,* in collaboration with Jake Saunders, and of two solo novels, *Them Bones* and *A Dozen Tough Jobs,* as well as the chapbook *A Better World's in Birth!.* He is at work on a new novel, tentatively entitled *The Moone World.* His most recent book is another new collection, *Horse of a Different Color.* He lives in Austin, Texas.

Beluthahatchie

ANDY DUNCAN

Everybody else got off the train at Hell, but I figured, it's a free country. So I commenced to make myself a mite more comfortable. I put my feet up and leaned back against the window, laid my guitar across my chest and settled in with my hat tipped down over my eyes, almost. I didn't know what the next stop was but I knew I'd like it better than Hell.

Whoo! I never saw such a mess. All that crowd of people jammed together on the Hell platform so tight you could faint standing up. One old battle-hammed woman hollering for Jesus, most everybody else just mumbling and crying and hugging their bags and leaning into each other and waiting to be told where to go. And hot? Man, I ain't just beating my gums there. Not as hot as the Delta, but hot enough to keep old John on the train. No, sir, I told myself, no room out there for me.

Fat old conductor man pushed on down the aisle kinda slow, waiting on me to move. I decided I'd wait on that, too.

"Hey, nigger boy." He slapped my foot with a rolled-up newspaper. Felt like the Atlanta paper. "This ain't no sleeping car."

"Git up off me, man. I ain't done nothing."

"Listen at you. Who you think you are, boy? Think you run the railroad? You don't look nothing like Mr. George Pullman." The conductor tried to put his foot up on the seat and lean on his knee, but he gave up with a grunt.

I ran one finger along my guitar strings, not hard enough to make a sound but just hard enough to feel them. "I ain't got a ticket, neither," I bit off, "but it was your railroad's pleasure to bring me this far, and it's my pleasure to ride on a little further, and I don't see what cause you got to be so astorperious about it, Mr. Fat Ass."

He started puffing and blowing. "What? What?" He was teakettle hot. You'd think I'd done something. "What did you call me, boy?" He whipped out a strap, and I saw how it was, and I was ready.

"Let him alone."

Another conductor was standing outside the window across the aisle, stooping over to look in. He must have been right tall and right big too, filling up the window like that. Cut off most of the light. I couldn't make out his face, but I got the notion that pieces of it was sliding around, like there wan't quite a face ready to look at yet. "The Boss will pick him up at the next stop. Let him be."

"The Boss?" Fat Ass was getting whiter all the time.

"The Boss said it would please him to greet this nigger personally."

Fat Ass wan't studying about me anymore. He slunk off, looking back big-eyed at the man outside the window. I let go my razor and let my hand creep up out of my sock, slow and easy, making like I was just shifting cause my leg was asleep.

The man outside hollered: "Board! All aboard! Next stop, Beluthahatchie!"

That old mama still a-going. "Jesus! Save us, Jesus!"

"All aboard for Beluthahatchie!"

"Jesus!"

We started rolling out.

"All aboard!"

"Sweet Je—" And her voice cut off just like that, like the squawk of a hen Meemaw would snatch for Sunday dinner. Wan't my business. I looked out the window as the scenery picked up speed. Wan't nothing to see, just fields and ditches and swaybacked mules and people stooping and picking, stooping and picking, and by and by a porch with old folks sitting on shuck-bottomed chairs looking out at all the years that ever was, and I thought I'd seen enough of all that to last me a while. Wan't any of my business at all.

When I woke up I was lying on a porch bench at another station, and hanging on one chain was a blown-down sign that said Beluthahatchie. The sign wan't swinging cause there wan't no breath of air. Not a soul else in sight neither. The tracks ran off into the fields on both ends as far as I could see, but they was all weeded up like no train been through since the Surrender. The windows over my head was boarded up like the bank back home. The planks along the porch han't been swept in years by nothing but the wind, and the dust was in whirly patterns all around.

Still lying down, I reached slowly beneath the bench, groping the air, till I heard, more than felt, my fingers pluck a note or two from the strings of my guitar. I grabbed it by the neck and sat up, pulling the guitar into my lap and hugging it, and I felt some better.

Pigeons in the eaves was a-fluttering and a-hooting all mournful-like, but I couldn't see 'em. I reckon they was pigeons. Meemaw used to say that pigeons sometimes was the souls of dead folks let out of Hell. I didn't think those folks back in Hell was flying noplace, but I did feel something was wrong, bad wrong, powerful wrong. I had the same crawly feeling as before I took that fatal swig—when Jar Head Sam, that harp-playing bastard, passed me a poisoned bottle at a Mississippi jook joint and I woke up on that one-way train.

Then a big old hound dog ambled around the corner of the station on my left, and another big old hound dog ambled around the comer of the station on my right. Each one was nearbouts as big as a calf and so fat it could hardly go, swanking along with its belly on the planks and its nose down. When the dogs snuffled up to the bench where I was sitting, their legs give out and they flopped down, yawned, grunted, and went fast to sleep like they'd been poleaxed. I could see the fleas hopping across their big butts. I started laughing.

"Lord, the hellhounds done caught up to me now! I surely must have led them a chase, I surely must. Look how wore out they are!" I hollered and cried, I was laughing so hard. One of them broke wind real long, and that set me off again. "Here come the brimstone! Here come the sulfur! Whoo! Done took my breath. Oh, Lordy." I wiped my eyes.

Then I heard two way-off sounds, one maybe a youngun dragging a stick along a fence, and the other maybe a car motor.

"Well, shit," I said.

Away off down the tracks, I saw a little spot of glare vibrating along in the sun. The flappity racket got louder and louder. Some fool was driving his car along on the tracks, a bumpety-bump, a bumpety-bump. It was a Hudson Terraplane, right sporty, exactly like what Peola June used to percolate around town in, and the chrome on the fender and hood was shining like a conk buster's hair.

The hound dogs was sitting up now, watching the car. They was stiff and still on each side of my bench, like deacons sitting up with the dead.

When the car got nigh the platform it lurched up out of the cut, gravel spitting, gears grinding, and shut off in the yard at the end of the porch where I was sitting. Sheets of dust sailed away. The hot engine ticked. Then the driver's door opened, and out slid the devil. I knew him well. Time I saw him slip down off the seat and hitch up his pants, I knew.

He was a sunburnt, bandy-legged, pussel-gutted li'l peckerwood. He wore braces and khaki pants and a dirty white undershirt and a big derby hat that had white hair flying out all around it like it was attached to the brim, like if he'd tip his hat to the ladies his hair would come off too.

He had a bright-red possum face, with beady, dumb black eyes and a long sharp nose, and no chin at all hardly and a big goozlum in his neck that jumped up and down like he couldn't swallow his spit fast enough. He slammed the car door and scratched himself a little, up one arm and then the other, then up one leg till he got to where he liked it. He hunkered down and spit in the dust and looked all unconcerned like maybe he was waiting on a tornado to come along and blow some victuals his way, and he didn't take any more notice of me than the hound dogs had.

I wan't used to being treated such. "You keep driving on the tracks thataway, hoss," I called, "and that Terraplane gone be butt-sprung for sure."

He didn't even look my way. After a long while, he stood up and leaned on a fender and lifted one leg and looked at the bottom of his muddy clodhopper, then put it down and lifted the other and looked at it too. Then he hitched his pants again and headed across the yard toward me. He favored his right leg a little and hardly picked up his feet at all when he walked. He left ruts in the yard like a plow. When he reached the steps, he didn't so much climb 'em as stand his bantyweight self on each one and look proud, like each step was all his'n now, and then go on to claim the next one too. Once on the porch, he sat down with his shoulders against a post, took off his hat and fanned himself. His hair had a better hold on his head than I thought, what there was of it. Then he pulled out a stick and a pocketknife and commenced to whittle. But he did all these things so deliberate and thoughtful that it was almost the same as him talking, so I kept quiet and waited for the words to catch up.

"It will be a strange and disgraceful day unto this world," he finally said, "when I ask a gut-bucket nigger guitar player for advice on autoMObile mechanics, or for anything else except a tune now and again." He had eyes like he'd been shot twice in the face. "And furthermore, I am the Lord of Darkness and the Father of Lies, and if I want to drive my 1936 Hudson Terraplane, with its six-cylinder seventy-horsepower engine, out into the middle of some loblolly and shoot out its tires and rip up its seats and piss down its radiator hole, why, I will do it and do it again seven more times afore breakfast, and the voice that will stop me will not be yourn. You hearing me, John?"

"Ain't my business," I said. Like always, I was waiting to see how it was.

"That's right, John, it ain't your business," the devil said. "Nothing I do is any of your business, John, but everything you do is mine. I was there the night you took that fatal drink, John. I saw you fold when your gut bent double on you, and I saw the shine of your blood coming up. I saw that whore you and Jar Head was squabbling over doing business at your funeral. It was a sorry-ass death of a sorry-ass man, John, and I had a big old time with it."

The hound dogs had laid back down, so I stretched out and rested my feet on one of them. It rolled its eyes up at me like its feelings was hurt.

"I'd like to see old Jar Head one more time," I said. "If he'll be along directly, I'll wait here and meet his train."

"Jar Head's plumb out of your reach now, John," the devil said, still whittling. "I'd like to show you around your new home this afternoon. Come take a tour with me."

"I had to drive fifteen miles to get to that jook joint in the first place," I said, "and then come I don't know how far on the train to Hell and past it. I've done enough traveling for one day."

"Come with me, John."

"I thank you, but I'll just stay here."

"It would please me no end if you made my rounds with me, John." The stick he was whittling started moving in his hand. He had to grip it a little to hang on, but he just kept smiling. The stick started to bleed along the cuts, welling up black red as the blade skinned it. "I want to show off your new home place. You'd like that, wouldn't you, John?" The blood curled down his arm like a snake.

I stood up and shook my head real slow and disgusted, like I was bored by his conjuring, but I made sure to hold my guitar between us as I walked past him. I walked to the porch steps with my back to the devil, and I was headed down them two at a time when he hollered out behind, "John! Where do you think you're going?"

I said real loud, not looking back: "I done enough nothing for one day. I'm taking me a tour. If your ass has slipped between the planks and got stuck, I'll fetch a couple of mules to pull you free."

I heard him cuss and come scrambling after me with that leg a-dragging, sounding just like a scarecrow out on a stroll. I was holding my guitar closer to me all the time.

I wan't real surprised that he let those two hound dogs ride up on the front seat of the Terraplane like they was Mrs. Roosevelt, while I had to walk in the road alongside, practically in the ditch. The devil drove real slow, talking to me out the window the whole time.

"Whyn't you make me get off the train at Hell, with the rest of those sorry people?"

"Hell's about full," he said. "When I first opened for business out here, John, Hell wan't no more'n a wide spot in the road. It took a long time to get any size on it. When you stole that dime from your poor old Meemaw to buy a French post card and she caught you and flailed you across the yard, even way back then, Hell wan't no bigger'n Baltimore. But it's about near more'n I can handle now, I tell you. Now I'm filling up towns all over these parts. Ginny Gall. Diddy-Wah-Diddy. West Hell—I'd run out of ideas when I named West Hell, John."

A horsefly had got into my face and just hung there. The sun was fierce, and my clothes was sticking to me. My razor slid hot along my ankle. I kept favoring my guitar, trying to keep it out of the dust as best I could.

"Beluthahatchie, well, I'll be frank with you, John, Beluthahatchie ain't much of a place. I won't say it don't have possibilities, but right now it's mostly just that railroad station, and a crossroads, and fields. One long, hot, dirty field after another." He waved out the window at the scenery and grinned. He had yellow needly teeth. "You know your way around a field, I reckon, don't you, John?"

"I know enough to stay out of 'em."

His laugh was like a man cutting tin. "I swear you are a caution, John. It's a wonder you died so young."

We passed a right lot of folks, all of them working in the sun. Pulling tobacco. Picking cotton. Hoeing beans. Old folks scratching in gardens. Even younguns carrying buckets of water with two hands, slopping nearly all of it on the ground afore they'd gone three steps. All the people looked like they had just enough to eat to fill out the sad expression on their faces, and they all watched the devil as he drove slowly past. All those folks stared at me hard, too, and at the guitar like it was a third arm waving at 'em. I turned once to swat that blessed horsefly and saw a group of field hands standing in a knot, looking my way and pointing.

"Where all the white folks at?" I asked.

"They all up in heaven," the devil said. "You think they let niggers into heaven?" We looked at each other a long time. Then the devil laughed again. "You ain't buying that one for a minute, are you, John?"

I was thinking about Meemaw. I knew she was in heaven, if anyone was. When I was a youngun I figured she musta practically built the place, and had been paying off on it all along. But I didn't say nothing.

"No, John, it ain't that simple," the devil said. "Beluthahatchie's different for everybody, just like Hell. But you'll be seeing plenty of white folks. Overseers. Train conductors. Sheriff's deputies. If you get uppity, why, you'll see whole crowds of white folks. Just like home, John. Everything's the same. Why should it be any different?"

"'Cause you're the devil," I said. "You could make things a heap worse."

"Now, could I really, John? Could I really?"

In the next field, a big man with hands like gallon jugs and a pink splash across his face was struggling all alone with a spindly mule and a plow made out of slats. "Get on, sir," he was telling the mule. "Get on with you." He didn't even look around when the devil come chugging up alongside'

The devil gummed two fingers and whistled. "Ezekiel. Ezekiel! Come on over here, boy."

Ezekiel let go the plow and stumbled over the furrows, stepping high and clumsy in the thick dusty earth, trying to catch up to the Terraplane and not mess up the rows too bad. The devil han't slowed down any—in fact, I believe he had speeded up some. Left to his own doin's, the mule headed across the rows, the plow jerking along sideways behind him.

"Yessir?" Ezekiel looked at me sorta curious like, and nodded his head so slight I wondered if he'd done it at all. "What you need with me, boss?"

"I wanted you to meet your new neighbor. This here's John, and you ain't gone believe this, but he used to be a big man in the jook joints in the Delta. Writing songs and playing that dimestore git fiddle."

Ezekiel looked at me and said, "Yessir, I know John's songs." And I could tell he meant more than hearing them.

"Yes, John mighta been famous and saved enough whore money to buy him a decent instrument if he hadn't up and got hisself killed. Yes, John used to be one high-rolling nigger, but you ain't so high now, are you John?"

I stared at the li'l peckerwood and spit out: "High enough to see where I'm going, Ole Massa."

I heard Ezekiel suck in his breath. The devil looked away from me real casual and back to Ezekiel, like we was chatting on a veranda someplace.

"Well, Ezekiel, this has been a nice long break for you, but I reckon you ought to get on back to work now. Looks like your mule's done got loose." He cackled and speeded up the car. Ezekiel and I both walked a few more steps and stopped. We watched the back of the Terraplane getting smaller, and then I turned to watch his face from the side. I han't seen that look on any of my people since Mississippi.

I said, "Man, why do you all take this shit?"

He wiped his forehead with his wrist and adjusted his hat. "Why do you?" he asked. "Why do you, John?" He was looking at me strange, and when he said my name it was like a one-word sentence all its own.

I shrugged. "I'm just seeing how things are. It's my first day."

"Your first day will be the same as all the others, then. That sure is the story with me. How come you called him Ole Massa just now?"

"Don't know. Just to get a rise out of him, I reckon."

Away off down the road, the Terraplane had stopped, engine still running, and the little cracker was yelling. "John! You best catch up, John. You wouldn't want me to leave you wandering in the dark, now would you?"

I started walking, not in any gracious hurry though, and Ezekiel paced me. "I asked 'cause it put me in mind of the old stories. You remember those stories, don't you? About Ole Massa and his slave by name of John? And how they played tricks on each other all the time?"

"Meemaw used to tell such when I was a youngun. What about it?"

He was trotting to keep up with me now, but I wan't even looking his way. "And there's older stories than that, even. Stories about High John the Conqueror. The one who could-"

"Get on back to your mule," I said. "I think the sun has done touched you."

"—the one who could set his people free," Ezekiel said, grabbing my shoulder and swinging me around. He stared into my face like a man looking for something he's dropped and has got to find.

"John!" the devil cried.

We stood there in the sun, me and Ezekiel, and then something went out of his eyes, and he let go and walked back across the ditch and trudged after the mule without a word.

I caught up to the Terraplane just in time for it to roll off again. I saw how it was, all right.

A ways up the road, a couple of younguns was fishing off the right side of a plank bridge, and the devil announced he would stop to see had they caught anything, and if they had, to take it for his supper. He slid out of the Terraplane, with it still running, and the dogs fell out after him, a-hoping for a snack, I reckon. When the devil got hunkered down good over there with the younguns, facing the swift-running branch, I sidled up the driver's side of the car, eased my guitar into the back seat, eased myself into the front seat, yanked the thing into gear and drove off. As I went past I saw three round O's—a youngun and the devil and a youngun again.

It was a pure pleasure to sit down, and the breeze coming through the windows felt good too. I commenced to get even more of a breeze going, on that long, straightaway road. I just could hear the devil holler back behind:

"John! Get your handkerchief-headed, free-school Negro ass back here with my auto-MO-bile! Johhhhnnn!"

"Here I come, old hoss," I said, and I jerked the wheel and slewed that car around and barreled off back toward the bridge. The younguns and the dogs was ahead of the devil in figuring things out. The younguns scrambled up a tree as quick as squirrels, and the dogs went loping into a ditch, but the devil was all preoccupied, doing a salty jump and cussing me for a dadblasted blagstagging liver-lipped stormbuzzard, jigging around right there in the middle of the bridge, and he was still cussing when I drove full tilt onto that bridge and he did not cuss any less when he jumped clean out from under his hat and he may even have stepped it up some when he went over the side. I heard a ker-plunk like a big rock chunked into a pond just as I swerved to bust the hat with a front tire and then I was off the bridge and racing back the way we'd come, and that hat mashed in the road behind me like a possum.

I knew something simply awful was going to happen, but man! I slapped the dashboard and kissed my hand and slicked it back across my hair and said aloud, "Lightly, slightly, and politely." And I meant that thing. But my next move was to whip that razor out of my sock, flip it open and lay it on the seat beside me, just in case.

I came up the road fast, and from way off I saw Ezekiel and the mule planted in the middle of his field like rocks. As they got bigger I saw both their heads had been turned my way the whole time, like they'd started looking before I even came over the hill. When I got level with them I stopped, engine running, and leaned on the horn until Ezekiel roused himself and walked over. The mule followed behind, like a yard dog, without being cussed or hauled or whipped. I must have been a sight. Ezekiel shook his head the whole way. "Oh, John," he said. "Oh, my goodness. Oh, John."

"Jump in, brother," I said. "Let Ole Massa plow this field his own damn self."

Ezekiel rubbed his hands along the chrome on the side of the car, swiping up and down and up and down. I was scared he'd burn himself. "Oh, John." He kept shaking his head. "John tricks Ole Massa again. High John the Conqueror rides the Terraplane to glory."

"Quit that, now. You worry me."

"John, those songs you wrote been keeping us going down here. Did you know that?"

"I 'preciate it."

"But lemme ask you, John. Lemme ask you something before you ride off. How come you wrote all those songs about hellhounds and the devil and such? How come you was so sure you'd be coming down here when you died?"

I fidgeted and looked in the mirror at the road behind. "Man, I don't know. Couldn't imagine nothing else. Not for me, anyway."

Ezekiel laughed once, loud, boom, like a shotgun going off.

"Don't be doing that, man. I about jumped out of my britches. Come on and let's go."

He shook his head again. "Maybe you knew you was needed down here, John. Maybe you knew we was singing, and telling stories, and waiting." He stepped back into the dirt. "This is your ride, John. But I'll make sure everybody knows what you done. I'll tell 'em that things has changed in Beluthahatchie."

He looked off down the road. "You'd best get on. Shoot—maybe you can find some jook joint and have some fun afore he catches up to you."

"Maybe so, brother, maybe so."

I han't gone two miles afore I got that bad old crawly feeling. I looked over to the passengers' side of the car and saw it was all spattered with blood, the leather and the carpet and the chrome on the door, and both those mangy hound dogs was sprawled across the front seat wallowing in it, both licking my razor like it was something good, and that's where the blood was coming from, welling up from the blade with each pass of their tongues. Time I caught sight of the dogs, they both lifted their heads and went to howling. It wan't no howl like any dog should howl. It was more like a couple of panthers in the night.

"Hush up, you dogs!" I yelled. "Hush up, I say!"

One of the dogs kept on howling, but the other looked me in the eyes and gulped air, his jowls flapping, like he was fixing to bark, but instead of barking said:

"Hush yourself, nigger."

When I looked back at the road, there wan't no road, just a big thicket of bushes and trees a-coming at me. Then came a whole lot of screeching and scraping and banging, with me holding onto the wheel just to keep from flying out of the seat, and then the car went sideways and I heard an awful bang and a crack and then I didn't know anything else. I just opened my eyes later, I don't know how much later, and found me and my guitar lying on the shore of the Lake of the Dead.

I had heard tell of that dreadful place, but I never had expected to see it for myself. Preacher Dodds whispered to us younguns once or twice about it, and said you have to work awful hard and be awful mean to get there, and once you get there, there ain't no coming back. "Don't seek it, my children, don't seek it," he'd say.

As far as I could see, all along the edges of the water, was bones and carcasses and lumps that used to be animals—mules and horses and cows and coons and even little dried-up birds scattered like hickory chips, and some things lying away off that might have been animals and might not have been, oh Lord, I didn't go to look. A couple of buzzards was strolling the edge of the water, not acting hungry nor vicious but just on a tour, I reckon. The sun was setting, but the water didn't cast no shine at all. It had a dim and scummy look, so flat and still that you'd be tempted to try to walk across it, if any human could bear seeing what lay on the other side. "Don't seek it, my children, don't seek it." I han't sought it, but now the devil had sent me there, and all I knew to do was hold my guitar close to me and watch those buzzards a-picking and a-pecking and wait for it to get dark. And Lord, what would this place be like in the dark?

But the guitar did feel good up against me thataway, like it had stored up all the songs I ever wrote or sung to comfort me in a hard time. I thought about those field hands a-pointing my way, and about Ezekiel sweating along behind his mule, and the way he grabbed aholt of my shoulder and swung me around. And I remembered the new song I had been fooling with all day in my head while I was following that li'l peckerwood in the Terraplane.

"Well, boys," I told the buzzards, "if the devil's got some powers I reckon I got some, too. I didn't expect to be playing no blues after I was dead. But I guess that's all there is to play now. 'Sides, I've played worse places."

I started humming and strumming, and then just to warm up I played "Rambling on My Mind" cause it was, and "Sweet Home Chicago" cause I figured I wouldn't see that town no more, and "Terraplane Blues" on account of that damn car. Then I sang the song I had just made up that day.

> I'm down in Beluthahatchie, baby,
> Way out where the trains don't run
> Yes, I'm down in Beluthahatchie, baby,
> Way out where the trains don't run
> Who's gonna take you strolling now
> Since your man he is dead and gone

My body's all laid out mama
But my soul can't get no rest
My body's all laid out mama
But my soul can't get no rest
Cause you'll be sportin with another man
Lookin for some old Mr. Second Best

Plain folks got to walk the line
But the Devil he can up and ride
Folks like us we walk the line
But the Devil he can up and ride
And I won't never have blues enough
Ooh, to keep that Devil satisfied.

When I was done it was black dark and the crickets was zinging and everything was changed.

"You can sure get around this country," I said, "Just a-sitting on your ass."

I was in a cane-back chair on the porch of a little wooden house, with bugs smacking into an oil lamp over my head. Just an old cropper place, sitting in the middle of a cotton field, but it had been spruced up some. Somebody had swept the yard clean, from what I could see of it, and on a post above the dipper was a couple of yellow flowers in a nailed-up Chase & Sanborn can.

When I looked back down at the yard, though, it wan't clean anymore. There was words written in the dirt, big and scrawly like from someone dragging his foot.

DON'T GET A BIG HEAD JOHN
I'LL BE BACK

Sitting on my name was those two fat old hound dogs. "Get on with your damn stinking talking serves," I yelled, and I shied a rock at them. It didn't go near as far as I expected, just sorta plopped down into the dirt, but the hounds yawned and got up, snuffling each other, and waddled off into the dark.

I stood up and stretched and mumbled. But something was still shifting in the yard, just past where the light was. Didn't sound like no dogs, though.

"Who that? Who that who got business with a wore out dead man?"

Then they come up toward the porch a little closer where I could see. It was a whole mess of colored folks, men in overalls and women in aprons, granny women in bonnets pecking the ground with walking sticks, younguns with their bellies pookin out and no pants on, an old man with Coke-bottle glasses and his eyes swimming in your face nearly, and every last one of them grinning like they was touched. Why, Preacher Dodds woulda passed the plate and called it a revival. They massed up against the edge of the porch, crowding closer in and bumping up against each other, and reaching their arms out and taking hold of me, my lapels, my shoulders, my hands, my guitar, my face, the little ones aholt of my pants legs—not hauling on me or messing with me, just touching me feather light here and there like Meemaw used to touch her favorite quilt after she'd already folded it to put away. They was talking, too, mumbling and whispering and saying, "Here he is. We heard he was coming and here he is. God bless you friend, God bless you brother, God bless you son." Some of the womenfolks was crying, and there was Ezekiel, blowing his nose on a rag.

"Y'all got the wrong man," I said, directly, but they was already heading back across the yard, which was all churned up now, no words to read and no pattern neither. They was looking back at me and smiling and touching, holding hands and leaning into each other, till they was all gone and it was just me and the crickets and the cotton.

Wan't nowhere else to go, so I opened the screen door and went on in the house. There was a bed all turned down with a feather pillow, and in the middle of the checkered oilcloth on the table was a crock of molasses, a jar of buttermilk, and a plate covered with a rag. The buttermilk was cool like it had been chilling in the well, with water beaded up on the sides of the jar. Under the rag was three hoecakes and a slab of bacon.

When I was done with my supper, I latched the front door, lay down on the bed and was just about dead to the world when I heard something else out in the yard—swish, swish, swish. Out the window I saw, in the edge of the porch light, one old granny woman with a shuck broom, smoothing out the yard where the folks had been. She was sweeping it as clean as for company on a Sunday. She looked up from under her bonnet and showed me what teeth she had and waved from the wrist like a youngun, and then she backed on out of the light, swish swish swish, rubbing out her tracks as she went.

First published in *Asimov's Science Fiction Magazine,* March 1997.

Andy Duncan made his first sale in 1997. By the beginning of the new century, he was widely recognized as one of the most individual, quirky, and flavorful new voices on the scene today. His story "The Executioner's Guild" was on both the Final Nebula Ballot and the final ballot for the World Fantasy Award in 2000, and in 2001 he won two World Fantasy Awards, for his story "The Pottawatomie Giant," and for his landmark first collection, *Beluthahatchie and Other Stories.* He also won the Theodore Sturgeon Memorial Award in 2002 for his novella "The Chief Designer." His other books include an anthology co-edited with F. Brett Cox, *Crossroads: Tales of the Southern Literary Fantastic,* and a non-fiction guidebook, Alabama Curiosities. His most recent books include a chapbook novella, *The Night Cache,* and a new collection, *The Pottawatomie Giant and Other Stories.* A graduate of the Clarion West writers' workshop in Seattle, he was born in Batesberg, South Carolina, now lives in Frostburg, Maryland with his wife Sydney, and is an Assistant Professor in the Department of English at Frostburo State University.

From Wooden Legs to Carbon Fiber Hands: How Technology Improves Prosthetic Limbs

ED GRABIANOWSKI

Humans are incredibly adaptable. A person can lose a hand or a leg and learn how to do most of the same things they could do before, from mundane daily tasks to impressive athletic feats. No one would argue that life is easier when you've lost a limb though, which is why we've been making, using, and improving prosthetic limbs for thousands of years.

The earliest prosthetics were rudimentary limbs made of bundled fibers, wood, or metal. The Roman General Marcus Sergius was said to have worn an iron hand circa 200 BC. These limbs were attached with straps and harnesses, and didn't offer much functionality—a wooden leg might offer balance and slow walking with a cane, but an iron hand or prosthetic arm was mostly just cosmetic.

Prosthetic limb technology advanced slowly, but the development of better attachment systems, lighter materials, and more effective control mechanisms improved life for those who had lost limbs or were born without them. Major advancements were often driven by sudden influxes of wounded soldiers who lost limbs in the world's most cataclysmic wars. For instance, the number of amputees coming home from Civil War battlefields drove researchers to create several new types of artificial limbs, including the Hanger Limb and William Selpho's prosthetic arm.

Selpho's design is particularly significant because it included one of the early control mechanisms, offering something beyond a simple static hook. A strap running to the opposite shoulder could be pulled taught by shrugging or otherwise moving the shoulder, activating a mechanism in the prosthetic hand that caused the fingers to close and open. While prosthetic technology seemed to creep forward for the last few hundred years, it's clear that important work was being done, and the advances helped improve lives.

Advances in the last decade, however, have moved with astonishing speed. New materials like titanium and carbon fiber make today's prosthetics lighter, which brings a host of add-on benefits like greater freedom of movement, reduced user fatigue, and a wider variety of attachment options. Cutting edge control mechanisms are far beyond anything Selpho could have imagined, incorporating muscle impulses or even brain-computer interfaces.

One of the exciting things about prosthetic development is that it incorporates so many scientific disciplines. Medical science works with the prosthetic wearer's physiology and the underlying tissues of a residual limb. Materials science and engineering play a major role in development. Practical nuts and bolts mechanical know-how is important too. Computer science has taken on a vital role with the development of more advanced control systems. While this may have once created barriers to smooth, efficient development, researchers and people involved with open source prosthetic projects can take advantage of the Internet to share information and build off of each other's work.

Materials

Advanced plastics have improved the cosmetic appearance of prostheses for those who desire a natural appearance. Shells and covers can be carefully matched to the wearer's skin tone, and expert painting can capture the look of real skin.

The biggest breakthrough in prosthetic materials has been carbon fiber. Carbon fiber is significantly stronger than steel while weighing much less. It's made of fine carbon filaments, which are woven into larger fibers, made into fabric and laminated with epoxy resin into rigid shapes. Its properties allow it to be constructed into shapes that bend and rebound, acting like springs. The best-known example is the Flex-Foot Cheetah, a carbon fiber prosthetic leg that looks like a curved "blade." Many para-athletes use these legs, which allow them to run with a natural gait at high speeds.

The lightness of carbon fiber allows prosthetic limbs to be attached with suction or with ratcheting devices that are much more comfortable and easy to use than earlier strap systems. A split-toe carbon fiber foot flexes naturally, increasing the wearer's agility and the naturalness of his or her gait.

Control Methods

No aspect of prosthetic science has developed as much, or become as complex, as control methods. Lower limb prosthetics are somewhat simpler because the wearer can control it without any kind of command-response mechanism. A good example of this is the Rheo Knee. A human knee is not a simple hinge that flops along as you swing your legs. Through complex muscular controls you may not be aware exist, the stiffness and angle of your knee varies depending on your walking speed, the surface you're traversing, and even where you are in your stride. The Rheo Knee uses microcomputers to measure the load and angle experienced by the knee. It then adjusts the stiffness of the joint by altering the viscosity of a magnetic fluid. Another common prosthetic, the C-Leg, also provides computer controlled dynamic stiffness adjustments. The result is not only a more natural gait, but the wearer has an easier time walking because the leg properly transfers momentum during the various phases of a stride.

The next step in control mechanisms involves myoelectrics. A myoelectric system gives the wearer direct control over some of the prosthesis' movements, the degree of which largely depends on the tissue and muscle left in the residual limb. Those muscles still receive signals from the brain when a command to move the limb is issued, even though the limb is no longer there. Normally, those nerve signals dead-end, but myoelectric sensors pick up those signals and interpret them into controlled movements of a prosthetic limb. In some cases, nerves are surgically rerouted to send signals to different existing muscles.

To use a myoelectric limb, the wearer has to undergo some training, and the device must be adjusted until they "learn" how to work together. By tensing specific muscles, the wearer can induce specific movements in the prosthetic. Different intensities of the same muscle can create different movements. These commands can be built up into very complex movements, including sequential finger movements or large shoulder motions. Even in cases where nerve damage or a lack of sufficient remaining muscle in the residual limb would prevent myoelectric operation, muscles in the chest and back can be used instead.

Myoelectric arms and hands are already on the market. The bebionic3 hand and a number of elbow, wrist and hand mechanisms from Ottobock are just a few examples. Myoelectric legs provide even greater freedom of movement compared to a dynamic leg like the Rheo Knee, because the wearer can activate motors to lift the leg up stairs or even adjust it while sitting without manually moving the leg by hand.

The concept of myoelectrics ultimately leads to brain-computer interfaces. If the control system for our muscles is really just a network of signals and relays, why not cut out the relays and go directly to the command center? This may be necessary because a spinal injury prevents any nerve signals from moving through the body, making myoelectric control impossible.

Whenever something happens in your brain, whether you're reflecting on a memory or deciding to make a fist, electric signals are generated as the ions in each neuron create a difference in electrical potential. These signals can be read either by electrodes inserted surgically into the brain or by electrodes attached to the scalp. There are problems with both methods. The signals are quite tiny, and your skull is a pretty good insulator, so scalp electrodes can pick up crosstalk or just have a hard time getting a reading.

Implanted electrodes get better signals, but of course they require invasive surgery. They need to be placed in the correct place within the brain to read the signals necessary to control a device. Unfortunately your brain is not an unchanging thing—over time it grows and shifts so that the implanted electrodes slowly migrate away from where they need to be.

While controlling prosthesis with the mind is an enticing idea, and one with enormous potential, there are a lot of difficulties with brain-computer interfaces. We're probably a few decades away from the kind of smoothly responsive, accurate and effective control you might see in a science-fiction story.

Sensory Feedback

Controlling a prosthetic limb has been a one-way street for many years. The wearer issues a command, the limb receives the signal and performs the task. Only recently has progress been made to send signals the other way, giving the prosthesis a sense of touch. This would allow the wearer to experience someone holding his or her hand, or more easily accomplish tasks like reaching into a bag to grab an apple instead of a pencil. It's also very important for fine tasks like holding a delicate object. Research in this area is not as well developed as controlling a limb, but DARPA's FINE (flat interface nerve electrode) already shows a great deal of promise.

Open Source

There are three primary reasons for the rapid advance of prosthetic technology in recent years. Increased availability and expertise in working with carbon fiber, along with improvements in carbon fiber manufacturing that make it easier and less expensive to work with, have had a huge impact. Another major factor is DARPA (Defense Advanced Research Projects Agency) initiated their Revolutionizing Prosthetics program in 2006, spurred in large part by the large number of soldiers returning from Middle Eastern conflicts with amputation injuries. Research backed by DARPA support and funding produced several commercially viable prosthetic systems, and major advances in brain control.

The third factor might be the most exciting—open source prosthetics. Prosthetic wearers have always tinkered with and improved on their limbs, of course, but there was never a method of easily sharing what they'd learned or made, and no framework for working on projects together. The open source concept, in which designs are shared freely with the public so they can be used, adapted, and improved upon, has pushed prosthetic design in new directions and helped push down prices.

A quick look around the various community projects ongoing at The Open Prosthetics Project shows an astonishing array of development. One group found that plastic zip ties make excellent artificial tendons. Another is using Lego building blocks to prototype hand designs. A project to improve attachment methods (called "suspensions") hit upon the idea of the Chinese finger puzzle: a sleeve open at each end that grabs onto a finger (or, for instance, an arm stump) with greater strength the harder it's pulled due to the alignment of fibers within the sleeve. Their early experiments have been promising. Yet another group found a few versions of a classic "split hook" artificial hand that is no longer produced. They hope to reverse engineer it and make new, cheaper versions with modern materials.

If the progress of prosthetics follows a predictable arc, we'll see artificial limbs get lighter and stronger in the coming years, as control methods become more reliable and sensory feedback more lifelike. But the most important advance might be making quality prosthetics less expensive. An advanced prosthetic leg or arm can cost tens of thousands of dollars, and few insurance policies will cover the price.

Open source holds a lot of promise. However, advanced prosthetics will remain out of financial reach for most of the people with amputation injuries or congenital limb problems. There are several charity and outreach organizations, including the Limbs for Life Foundation and the Amputee Coalition. The Open Prosthetics Project even has a wiki page with information on getting financial assistance to buy a prosthetic limb.

In Kansas City, a young boy with congenital deformity of his right hand couldn't afford a commercially produced prosthetic. A local teen used shared files by the open source community to create a hand using the local library's 3D printer, then assembled the hand for the young boy to use. The hand's designers even adapted the design to fit the boy. It's certainly a heartwarming story, but it's also a great example of the benefits of open source prosthetics.

ABOUT THE AUTHOR

Ed Grabianowski writes for sites like *HowStuffWorks* and *io9* about science, technology, games, and anything else that looks interesting. His fiction has been published in *Black Static* and the *Geek Love* anthology.

The Immense Costs and a Shred of Optimism: A Conversation with L. E. Modesitt, Jr.

JEREMY L. C. JONES

Cyador's Heirs, a novel of five hundred and twelve pages, begins with a boy and a girl sitting in awkward silence. Two guards watch them and two more guards watch those guards. The detail is fine and the prose discreet:

The boy and the girl sit on a carved wooden bench in the shade beside the small courtyard fountain. He has pale white skin, unruly red hair and a strong straight nose just short of being considered excessive. Her hair is black, as are her eyes, and her skin is smooth, if the light tan of aged parchment. Her name is Kyedra. His is Lerial.

Kyedra breaks the silence with a question. There is a slight language barrier, and more questions. They discuss differences in their customs and the tensions between their cultures.

So gently, it begins . . .

Cyador's Heirs by L. E. Modesitt, Jr. is the seventeenth novel in The Saga of the Recluce Series but it offers an entry point for newcomers, set as it is, after the fall of Cyador, at a time of re-building, at a time when the younger generation must reap the past.

L. E. Modesitt, Jr. started out with poetry and non-fiction and has been writing fiction since the early 70s. Modesitt has a rich professional history as, among other things, a Navy pilot, a staff director for a U.S. Congressman, and Director of Legislation and Congressional Relations for the U.S. Environmental Protection Agency. His careers in the military and politics serve as distant background sources for his complex novels.

All in all, Modesitt is the author of more than five dozen fantasy and science fiction novels. His series include The Imager Portfolio, The Corean Chronicles Series, The Ecolitan Matter Series, The Forever Hero Series, The Ghost Books Series, The Saga of Recluce Series, The Spellsong Cycle Series, Timegods' World Series. His standalone novels include *Haze, Empress of Eternity,* and last year's *The One-Eyed Man.* His novels are long and multi-layered with extensive casts of complex character, yet they remain, line for line, intimate and brightly lit.

Below, Modesitt and I talk about *Cyador's Heirs,* writing, and his work in progress.

What are some of your favorite moments in *Cyador's Heirs?*

I can't say that I have favorite parts, per se. What aspect of the book that I like is how much Lerial changes from the beginning to the end without really understanding how much better a person he has become, even as he recognizes the sometimes ruthless imperatives and cruel choices required in good governing.

Does writing a novel answer or present more questions for you?

I think it's more that I'm trying to answer existing questions about life, technology/magic, human nature, society, government in a way that tells a good story and makes sense in life while providing both a sense of the immense costs and a shred of optimism. My characters do generally achieve their goals/dreams, but the costs are far higher than they ever thought possible at the beginning of their journey, and they also learn more than they anticipated, learning that is not always welcome or pleasant.

Do you ever lose that "shred of optimism?" Are the costs ever too high for you? For your characters?

I try not to lose that shred of optimism, but I'd have to say that there isn't much optimism in the ending of *In Endless Twilight*, the last book of *The Forever Hero*. And I think that I would personally have great difficulty paying the costs incurred and paid by some of my protagonists.

Do you approach series novels differently from standalones? Is one easier than the other?

Every book is a challenge, if in different ways. For my fantasy series books, particularly in starting the first book, I need to do a broad scope of work, dealing with history and background, culture, economics, geography [and yes, maps], the magic system, and societal beliefs. This is critical because readers will question the slightest possibility of inconsistency. In writing a stand-alone, the scope is just as broad, but the depth is less, because I have to convey being part of a larger universe in a less expansive canvas.

What were some of the challenges specific to writing *Cyador's Heirs*? Do you set out to challenge yourself? Do the challenges arise?

The most specific challenge to writing *Cyador's Heirs* lay in the fact that it is a part of the Saga of Recluce, and that the books in the saga span almost two-thousand years. Because I did not write the books in chronological order, by now every reader of the saga knows at least parts of the general history of the world. So each additional volume that fills in blank or fuzzy areas of that history has to be written to be consistent with that history and fit in with all the cultures that have risen and fallen while still presenting an exciting story while revealing and adding yet another intriguing facet in the twisting balance between lands, and between order and chaos.

I always attempt to do something different with every book I write. That's one challenge, and in doing that, there are others that inevitably arise.

In what ways, if any, has your creative process changed in the last forty years?

When I first started writing prose, I wrote short stories, literally off the top of my head, pretty much start to finish. Needless to say, my sales percentage was less than sterling. When I started to write novels, that didn't work, and I began to write mosaic fashion, which interestingly enough helped for two reasons. First, it caused me to think out ahead, and, second, it allowed me to avoid getting hung up at any one point. As I've become more experienced, I write more than before in a straight line of narrative, but I haven't abandoned writing sections that will come later in a book. For the last twenty-one years, I've been a full-time writer, and that has meant that I devote most of each day to some aspect of writing. The change in the marketplace has meant that I also spend more time on an internet presence and in creating content for my website [lemodesittjr. com] and in doing more marketing in various ways.

What have been some of your personal landmarks throughout your career?

In a way, the first landmark was even writing my first SF story. I'd been struggling for over ten years as a poet, getting published only in very small magazines, when someone suggested I write a science fiction story. The second landmark came six years later when Ben Bova, then editor of *Analog*, rejected a story and told me he wouldn't buy another until I went and wrote a novel, which was very good advice, given that, so far, I've sold every novel I've written. The third was writing *The Magic of Recluce*, which I did as a reaction to existing fantasy books which displayed no understanding of basic human society, economics, technology, or government, and which laid the foundation for my success as a fantasy writer. Others include writing *The Soprano Sorceress*, my first book from the female point of view, *Archform:Beauty*, my first book from multiple viewpoints with distinctly different linguistic patterns for each viewpoint; getting a book rejected for a movie by James Cameron because it was "too complex"; making the *New York Times* bestseller list with books in two different fantasy series.

Are you having as much fun as it seems like you're having? And what're the fun part of writing? The not-so-fun parts?

For me, writing isn't "fun." It is immensely satisfying, especially those moments when I feel that I got something "just right." But then, I've never been a toy-boy or a "fun" type, perhaps because what matters most to me is accomplishment and understanding, and the appreciation and creation of beauty, not only in what I do, but in what others do as well. There's certainly more of a sense of satisfaction and accomplishment when I've finished the final draft and it's ready to go to the editor than when the book is actually published. The very necessary but not-so-fun parts are going over copyedits and especially first pass galleys.

Would you be willing to discuss specific novels, stories, or elements in the works of others that you find beautiful?

I'd rather not, because I can think of quite a number of elements in the works of others that I find beautiful, and limiting myself to what is likely to be printed would single out, unfairly, I believe, those I could mention within the reasonable space and time limitations, and by comparison suggest that those I did not mention were of lesser beauty.

How do you go about creating characters?

I have an image of a character early on. That image begins to form when I'm in the process of thinking about the culture, society, climate, and all the other background aspects of the book I'm writing. Part of that comes from my own background. Because it took more than twenty years from the time I sold my first story, and more than thirty from the time my first poem was published, before I was successful enough as a writer to write full-time, I spent almost thirty years in full-time employment doing jobs other than writing fiction, from time in the Navy as an amphibious boat officer to a search and rescue helicopter pilot, a professional economist, and a political staffer in Washington, D.C., not to mention a number of other jobs in which I was far less successful. That kind of experience gives me a lot to draw on, as well as the understanding of the personality traits that make people successful or less so in various fields.

Are there certain moments in* Cyador's Heirs *that are particularly meaningful to you?

In one part of the book, Lerial makes a miscalculation, understandably enough, given that he's sixteen and not very experienced in battle, and that miscalculation leads to a death that could have been avoided. The person who died was a relative of a high official . . . and Lerial has to explain in person exactly what happened. That part had a particular meaning to me, which is very personal, given my own experiences as a Navy pilot.

What are you working on now and how is it challenging you?

I'm currently working on a comparatively "near-future" [for me, anyway, set a little over a century from now] hard SF novel that's about as science-intense as anything I've ever done. One of the plot points hinges on an extrapolation of a very recent astronomical discovery that hasn't gotten much press, but what it is . . . well, that will have to wait for when the book comes out, assuming, as always, that Tor decides to publish it.

Lastly, do you have any advice for young speculative fiction writers just starting out?

I've received a great deal of advice over the years, and I've probably given out almost as much, but the one thing that keeps coming back is that every single writer is different from every single other writer, and the key to writing successfully is to determine what works for you. This sounds simplistic, and doubtless some readers may claim that I'm avoiding the question. But while I have offered advice to individual writers over the years, that advice was based on what I knew that writer was doing . . . or failing to do.

While every successful writer I know has mastered the very basics of knowing solid grammar [mostly, anyway], having a wide knowledge base, and being able to write understandable sentences and paragraphs, beyond that they differ widely, and advice pertinent to one may not be useful to another . . . and at times, may be damaging. The two best pieces of writing advice I received were from Ben Bova, who told me to write novels at a time when I was struggling with short stories, and from Jim Tozzi, the head of the consulting firm for which I worked for a number of years, who said, after looking a policy paper I'd written for a client, "Where does it say our client is getting screwed? You wrote around that. If it doesn't the ***** say it, it doesn't say it. Go re-write it so it says so." I didn't use his exact language, but I did rewrite it, and I still recall his words.

Stories and novels have to have beginnings, middles, and ends, and in almost all cases they require characters and plots, but you don't have to write a story straight from beginning to end, and some good stories don't even end up in that order. Some writers know from the beginning what works for them, and some, regretfully, never do figure that out. The key is to keep doing and improving on what works and to change what doesn't.

ABOUT THE AUTHOR

Jeremy L. C. Jones is a freelance writer, editor, and teacher. He is the Staff Interviewer for *Clarkesworld Magazine* and a frequent contributor to *Kobold Quarterly* and *Booklifenow.com*. He teaches at Wofford College and Montessori Academy in Spartanburg, SC. He is also the director of Shared Worlds, a creative writing and world-building camp for teenagers that he and Jeff VanderMeer designed in 2006. Jones lives in Upstate South Carolina with his wife, daughter, and flying poodle.

Another Word:
Writers Tools
BUD SPARHAWK

In the good old days, long before everybody had pens and paper, story-tellers would just sit around the fire and spin tales, or repeat one told by others and adding some slight modifications to improve rhyme or meter. The only tools needed back then were a good memory and a lack of shame.

These days, a writer has software, hardware, and the intellectual wealth of the internet at their fingertips from which they can amass all of the background material they think they may need to write their stories. It's also a never-ending source of dangerously distracting amusements that are far more interesting than actually writing.

With the resources available and using some basic tools, anyone can easily craft a tale or repeat—albeit in different words—many-told stories. Whether or not a writer is successful in publishing what they craft depends largely on their ability to tell a compelling story and how well they use their tools.

The tools a writer selects depends a lot on the processes they use to build their tales. The specific tool is a matter of personal choice and temperament. Aside from pen and paper, computers, laptops, and tablets seem to appeal to many.

Writers also vary widely in the way they approach drafting and editing their work. This point was illustrated at the recent CapClave convention where Jamie Todd Rubin and I presented an On Line Writing Tools session.

We found that although we use some similar software, we employ them differently. For example, Jamie blogs frequently regarding his use of Evernote to support his writing process. He favors letting the story develop as it goes. I, on the other hand, prefer a more measured approach by setting the sequence of scenes in advance before writing the scene itself. The comparison of our methods was as illuminating for the audience as our descriptions of the tools themselves.

I started writing with WordPerfect, moved to MS Word, and later to Scrivener—one of the finest writer's tool ever developed, IMHO. I also use spreadsheets, databases, and the file features available on my operating system, such as categorizing, date sorting, etc.

I previously used a FileMaker Pro database with a home-built scene building application for stories under seven thousand words. This tool was quickly abandoned when I discovered I could build and manipulate scenes with an application called Scrivener. Being able to display scenes in a continuous and easy-to-follow thread was a godsend and reduced the endless cut and paste of word processors.

Scrivener is not the only arrow in my quiver. When I am away from my workstation, I use Internet Writer on my iPad to dash off a page or ten. At readings, I transfer the selection to my Kindle so I don't have to mess with paper, paper, paper or fumble with tiny (or missing) thumb drives.

Each tool that I've mentioned required developing a degree of familiarity and learning the skills needed to obtain the best results. Just as a chisel will not turn someone into a sculptor, a paint brush an artist, neither will any writing tool somehow grant a writer the magical powers of story creation. A writer has to keep in mind that their tools are only aids to let them concentrate on the most important aspect, which is to use their imagination and intelligence.

I've also designed network diagrams that show how scenes relate to one another, and, at times, created complex spreadsheets to supplement them. I also use Inspiration, a simple and inexpensive mind mapping tool, and a FileMaker Pro database for tracking my work and submissions. For the occasional collaboration I also use DropBox to share files.

I use all of the above on my home machine and usually work with multiple windows open, as illustrated on the next page.

Scrivener's wonderful corkboard continues to be my primary tool where I can display and manipulate my scene fragments. I can move scenes about, code them with color, and have as many open as I need. Scrivener also permits me to open reference windows containing useful facts—such as the names of the characters, settings, and progress of the work.

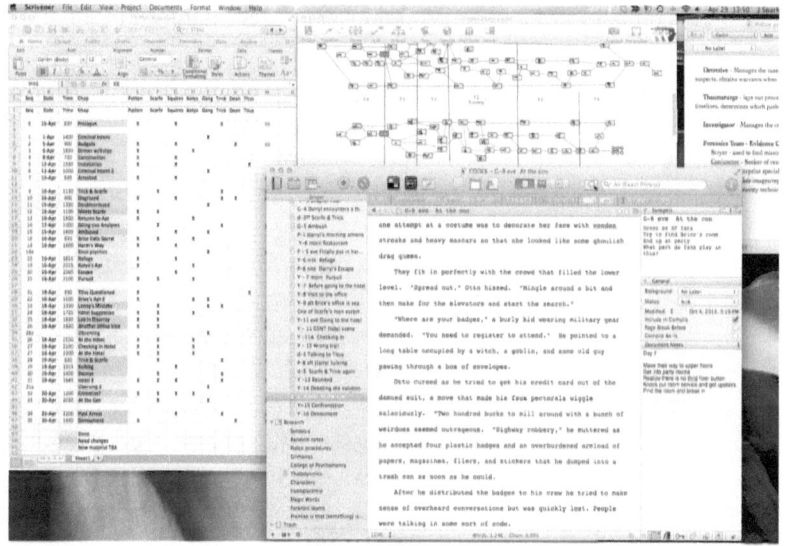

Beside the Scrivener features, I also keep my plot diagram open for quick reference and do the same with a spreadsheet. In the illustration above you can also see windows of my tracking database and file system peeking through the cracks.

Obviously this crowded screen did not arrive overnight and ready to use. I had to gradually discover the processes that worked best for me. I tried to devise a way to not lose the tenuous train of thought I had been following by needing to search elsewhere for something I needed. Better, I thought, to have it all there in front of me and instantly available.

But producing a finished manuscript is only a way to sell and/or publish it. To get it published an editor has to buy or reject it. Tracking what happens between you and all the assorted editors requires a type of tool.

To make an intelligent submission, a writer needs to know the publication's guidelines, their address or URL, the preferred length, and how soon they might expect a reply. Unless you carefully keep track of where your story sits, you might suffer the embarrassment of sending something back to an editor who has already read and rejected it.

Given the review cycles of most markets, there will be the inevitable delay as your precious manuscript gradually works its way to the top of the slush pile, into some editor's hands, and, if you are extremely lucky or gifted, into the final selection pile and onwards to publication.

This is valuable time, time you should be using to produce more stories, time that should be used in perfecting failed pieces, and time in which you should be sending out any rejected material to another market.

Serious writers keep their work in circulation until it either sells or the virtual ink wears off. As a consequence, any writer who is fairly productive has a number of manuscripts in circulation at any time. Sometimes this number will grow and, without some method of tracking, you might lose a manuscript and not even realize it, or discover that an unsent, completed story has been buried in the disaster of your computer filing system.

Index cards are a low-tech method for tracking but using a spreadsheet is as easy. More advanced yet is a database, which allows you both flexibility and content options not easily done on other methods, such as quickly finding all outstanding stories, or having the history of any piece instantly available. Another alternative is to use one of the many online tracking tools for your submissions list such as Duotrope, Writers, or many more, some of which are free or reasonably priced.

The secret of tracking is to decide in advance everything you might ever want to know about your manuscript. For example, I document when each piece originated, when it achieved its final, releasable form and, if necessary, when it was subsequently revised. I also record each editor and the dates submitted and when each replied. I live with the constant fear that I might lose track of which draft came first, which was the finished piece and how long it has been at a particular editor and an estimated reply date. Editors sometimes lose manuscripts, submissions occasionally go astray, and even fragile memory fades over time.

So don't wait, get your inventory of tools together now and start record keeping as an integral part of your writing schedule. A good set of tools will reward you, and perhaps leave a record of your work that far future biographer may value.

References

- Scrivener is an application that combines the features of a word processor with project management tools. The application allows a writer to outline the story, structure ideas, store and view research notes, and develop successive drafts while making all the above material quickly and easily available. You can find more information available at https://www.literatureandlatte.com/scrivener.php
- Inspiration is a relatively inexpensive mind-mapping tool that I use for thinking of how the various scenes tie together. In addition,

Inspiration has outline and work processing capabilities. You can find more information at http://www.inspiration.com

- FileMaker Pro is moderately priced and has a bit of a learning curve that can be bridged with the Dummy books. It lets you customize default screens, collect whatever data you wish, and even publish to the Internet. You can read more details at http://www.filemaker pro/
- Writer, or more properly The Internet Typewriter, is a free, cloud-based utility that does just what the name implies—type. This is no word processor, but it does cut out the need for file transfers, thumb drives, and other sneaker net methods. You can read more at https://writer.bighugelabs.com/
- DropBox is another cloud-based tool that is free for the basic setup. It provides what is essentially a spare drive for files. A copy can be downloaded from https://www.dropbox.com/install

ABOUT THE AUTHOR

Bud Sparhawk is a short story writer who has sold numerous science fiction stories to ANALOG, Asimov's, and other widely circulated magazines. He has been a three-time Nebula novella finalist. His work has appeared in several anthologies as well as print, audio, and on-line media both in the United States and overseas. His stories appear most frequently in Analog, less so in Asimov's and annually in the Defending the Future series of anthologies.

He has two print collections (Sam Boone: Front to Back and Dancing with Dragons,) one mass-market paperback (VIXEN), and several eBook collections and novels.

Bud is currently the Treasurer of SFWA and a member of SIGMA. He maintains a weekly blog on the writing life at budsparhawk.blogspot.com. A complete bibliography of stories, articles, and other material can be found at his web site.

Editor's Desk:
The Five Percent
NEIL CLARKE

I find writing an editorial to be a difficult task. I think this one remained a blank document for the first two weeks I tried to write it. Then the Hugo Award nominees were announced and suddenly I had something I could focus on. If you've been following this year's nominations and controversies surrounding some of the nominees, you already know that it has already provided countless blog fodder for people more eloquent than I. If you're looking for some more of that, prepare to be disappointed. Life is too short for me to be bothered with that.

What bothers me? As an editor and fan of short fiction, I'm bothered by the fact that we have less than five short story nominees for the third time in four years. This situation has been caused by a rule that requires nominees to have at least five percent of the nominations to make the final ballot. We won't know this year's nomination data until after the awards ceremony, but we have two other years that we can use to evaluate this rule.

Top Five 2013 Short Story Nominations

107—Immersion by Aliette de Bodard (16.6%)
38—Mono No Aware by Ken Liu (5.74%)
34—Mantis Wives by Kij Johnson (5.14%)
30—"No Place Like Home" by Seanan McGuire (4.53%)
28—"The Bookmaking Habits of Select Species" by Ken Liu (4.23%)
28—"Robot" by Helena Bell (4.23%)
28—"One Hell of a Ride" by Seanan McGuire (4.23%)
28—"We Will Not Be Undersold!" by Seanan McGuire (4.23%)

Top Five 2011 Short Story Nominations

72—The Things by Peter Watts (13.98%)
42—Ponies by Kij Johnson (8.16%)
29—Amaryllis by Carrie Vaughn (5.63%)
29—For Want of a Nail by Mary Robinette Kowal (5.63%)
25—Elegy for a Young Elk by Hannu Rajaniemi (4.85%)

One of the effects of the five percent rule is that it helps prevent an over-abundance of nominees in a category when there is a flat pool of nominations. In 2011, the rule eliminated one story and did not prevent a tie, but in 2013, it prevented a four-way tie for fifth place that would have resulted in eight nominations.

Some might argue that they should have allowed eight nominees, but I'm not among them. I think there is a value in trying to keep the number of nominations down. Looking at this data, however, I do see two people (Seanan McGuire for "No Place Like Home" and Hannu Rajaniemi for "Elegy for a Young Elk") that I think were unfairly stripped of their nominations by this rule.

When some people tried to first abolish and then fix the rules for Best Semiprozine, several of us stood up and got involved. That's the way this award works. Any fan can come to a WSFS business meeting and have a say in the rules. You can find the procedure documented on the Hugo Award's website at http://www.thehugoawards.org/changing-the-rules/.

Now I think it's time to fix the five percent rule so that we don't continue to deny otherwise eligible nominees the recognition fans would like to give them.

I've talked to a few people about possible work-arounds. A popular suggestion is to change the rule to use a "fixed number or five percent whichever is lower" instead of five percent. Unfortunately, that doesn't solve the problem. For example, to get five nominees in 2011, the number would have to be twenty-five, which would also give us eight nominees in 2013. We might pick a good number for past years, but it could be just as broken for a future year. No, a model that considers a minimum number of nominations will always have the potential to backfire.

The solution I'd like to put forward is to drop the five percent rule, place an upper cap of six nominees and instate a tie-breaker rule. In cases where there are seven or more, we simply eliminate works tied for the last available spot. For example, in 2013's four-way tie for fifth place, all four would be eliminated. There would have been four nominees, instead of the three allowed under the current rules. In 2011, these rules would have provided us with five nominees.

I believe this method of dealing with ties is closer to the spirit of the intent of the five percent rule than the actual rule has been in practice. If the number of people nominating for the Hugos continues to rise, I suspect the five percent rule will continue to go into effect and perhaps happen more often. I feel that we owe it to the nominees that have been (and will be) stripped of nominations to do something about this.

I'd love to have some feedback on this before I make any formal proposals. What do you think?

On a related note, I would like to congratulate this year's nominees and say thank you to everyone that nominated me for Best Editor Short Form. This is the third time I've been nominated in this category and I am so honored that you still consider me worthy!

ABOUT THE AUTHOR

Neil Clarke is the editor of *Clarkesworld Magazine,* owner of Wyrm Publishing and a current Hugo Award Nominee for Best Editor (short form). He currently lives in NJ with his wife and two children.

About the Artist

ALBERT URMANOV

Albert is a twenty-five year old artist from Anshero-Sudshensk, Russia. His passion for art manifested in school, where he would draw superhero fanart for his classmates. He later went on to become a designer for several media agencies and a freelance artist before landing his current job, an internship as a concept artist at Goodgame Studios in Hamburg. Aside from creating art, he enjoys aikido, anime, and hanging out with his wife and friends.

WEBSITE

albyu.cghub.com

www.ingramcontent.com/pod-product-compliance
Lightning Source LLC
Chambersburg PA
CBHW020544130626
46552CB00007B/2743